Mark Twain (Sa⋯⋯⋯⋯⋯⋯⋯⋯⋯⋯⋯⋯10)
was America's favo⋯⋯⋯⋯⋯⋯⋯⋯⋯⋯⋯⋯fty
years, he gathered ⋯⋯⋯⋯⋯⋯⋯⋯⋯⋯⋯⋯ from his experi-
ences. Growing up in Hannibal, Missouri, gave him the set-
ting for many of his writings, including *Tom Sawyer* and
The Adventures of Huckleberry Finn, which many people
consider to be his best books. He was a steamboat pilot, a
reporter on the western frontier, and a world traveler. Although he is famous for his novels, it was another type of
writing that first brought him literary success: his short stories.

Of about sixty short stories, Twain's most famous is "The
Celebrated Jumping Frog of Calaveras County," written
while on vacation in Calaveras County, California, and eagerly published in newspapers across the country. Rich in
frontier life and humor, it spurred him to a fame that con-
tinues beyond his death.

"The Story of the Bad Little Boy" shows the humorous
irony of how those who deserve punishment don't always
receive it.

"Is He Living or Is He Dead?" is a parody of the life of
starving artists and the one guarantee there is to fame in the
art world.

"The Man That Corrupted Hadleyburg" further explores
human nature, showing how greed can corrupt an entire
town. Twain's bitterness and disappointment in human nature is evident here.

"A Fable" is a brief study of point of view and, through
its animal characters, explores the old theory that one
doesn't have to see to believe.

Here we have the different phases of Twain: his opti-
mistic humor, his experienced satire, and his later contempt
for humanity.

MARK TWAIN

THE CELEBRATED JUMPING FROG AND OTHER STORIES

SCHOLASTIC INC.
New York Toronto London Auckland Sydney

ISBN 0-590-76370-9

12 11 10 9   7 8/0

Printed in the U.S.A.   01
First Scholastic printing, September 1997

CONTENTS

THE CELEBRATED
JUMPING FROG OF
CALAVERAS COUNTY

In compliance with the request of a friend of mine, who wrote me from the East, I called on good-natured, garrulous old Simon Wheeler, and inquired after my friend's friend, Leonidas W. Smiley, as requested to do, and I hereunto append the result. I have a lurking suspicion that *Leonidas W.* Smiley is a myth; that my friend never knew such a personage; and that he only conjectured that if I asked old Wheeler about him, it would remind him of his infamous *Jim* Smiley, and he would go to work and bore me to death with some exasperating reminiscence of him as long and as tedious as it should be useless to me. If that was the design, it succeeded.

I found Simon Wheeler dozing comfortably by the bar-room stove of the dilapidated tavern in the decayed mining camp of Angel's, and I noticed that he was fat and bald headed, and had an expression of winning gentleness and simplicity upon his tranquil countenance. He roused up, and gave me good day. I told him that a friend of mine had commissioned me to make some inquiries about a cherished companion of his boyhood named *Leonidas W.* Smiley — *Rev. Leonidas W.* Smiley, a young minister of the Gospel, who he had heard was at one time a resident of Angel's Camp. I added that if Mr. Wheeler could tell me anything about this Rev. Leonidas W. Smiley, I would feel under many obligations to him.

Simon Wheeler backed me into a corner and blockaded me there with his chair, and then sat down and reeled off the monotonous narrative which follows this paragraph. He never smiled, he never frowned, he never changed his voice from the gentle-flowing key to which he tuned his initial sentence, he never betrayed the slightest suspicion of enthusiasm; but all through the interminable narrative there ran a vein of impressive earnestness and sincerity, which showed me plainly that, so far from his imagining that there was anything ridiculous or funny about his story, he regarded it as a really important matter, and admired its two heroes as men of transcendent genius in *finesse*. I let him go on in his own way, and never interrupted him once.

"Rev. Leonidas W. H'm, Reverend Le — well, there was a feller here once by the name of *Jim* Smiley, in the winter of '49 — or maybe it was the spring of '50 — I don't recollect exactly, somehow, though what makes me think it was one or the other is because I remember the big flume warn't finished when he first come to the camp; but anyway, he was the curiousest man about always betting on anything that turned up you ever see, if he could get anybody to bet on the other side; and if he couldn't he'd change sides. Any way that suited the other man would suit *him* — any way just so's he got a bet, *he* was satisfied. But still he was lucky, uncommon lucky; he most always come out winner. He was always ready and laying for a chance; there couldn't be no solit'ry thing mentioned but that feller'd offer to bet on it, and take ary side you please, as I was just telling you. If there was a horse-race, you'd find him flush or you'd find him busted at the end of it; if there was a dog-fight, he'd bet on it; if there was a cat-fight, he'd bet on it; if there was a chicken-fight, he'd bet on it; why, if there was two birds set-ting on a fence, he would bet you which one would fly first; or if there was a camp-meeting, he would be there reg'lar to bet on Parson Walker, which he judged to be the best exhorter about here, and so he was too, and a good man. If he even see a straddle-bug start to go anywheres, he would bet you how long it would take him to get to — to wherever he was going to, and if you took him up, he would foller that straddle-bug to Mexico but what he would find out where he was bound for and how long he was on the road. Lots of the boys here has seen that Smiley, and can tell you about him. Why, it never made no diffcrence to *him* — he'd bet on *any* thing — the dangdest feller. Parson Walker's wife laid very sick once, for a good while, and it seemed as if they warn't going to save her; but one morning he come in, and Smiley up and asked him how she was, and he said she was considerable better — thank the Lord for his inf'nite mercy — and coming on so smart that with the blessing of Prov'dence she'd get well yet; and Smiley, before he thought, says, 'Well, I'll resk two-and-a-half she don't anyway.'

"Thish-yer Smiley had a mare — the boys called her the fifteen-minute nag, but that was only in fun, you know, because of course she was faster than that — and he used to win money on that horse, for all she was so slow and always had the asthma, or the distemper, or the consumption, or something of that kind. They used to give her two or three hundred yards' start, and then pass her under way; but always at the fag end of the race she'd get excited and desperate like, and come cavorting and straddling up, and scattering her legs around limber, sometimes in the air, and sometimes out to one side among the fences, and kicking up m-o-r-e dust and raising m-o-r-e racket with her coughing and sneezing and blowing her nose — and always fetch up at the stand just about a neck ahead, as near as you could cipher it down.

"And he had a little small bull-pup, that to look at him you'd think he warn't worth a cent but to set around and look ornery and lay for a chance to steal something. But as soon as money was up on him he was a different dog; his under-jaw'd begin to stick out like the fo'castle of a steamboat, and his teeth would uncover and shine like the furnaces. And a dog might tackle him and bully-rag him, and bite him, and throw him over his shoulder two or three times, and Andrew Jackson — which was the name of the pup — Andrew Jackson would never let on but what *he* was satisfied, and hadn't expected nothing else — and the bets being doubled and doubled on the other side all the time, till the money was all up; and then all of a sudden he would grab that other dog jest by the j'int of his hind leg and freeze to it — not chaw, you understand, but only just grip and hang on till they throwed up the sponge, if it was a year. Smiley always come out winner on that pup, till he harnessed a dog once that didn't have no hind legs, because they'd been sawed off in a circular saw, and when the thing had gone along far enough, and the money was all up, and he come to make a snatch for his pet holt, he see in a minute how he'd been imposed on, and how the other dog had him in the door, so to speak, and he 'peared surprised, and then he looked sorter discouraged-like, and didn't try no more to win the fight, and so he got shucked out bad. He give Smiley a look, as much as to say his heart was broke, and it was *his* fault, for putting up a dog that hadn't no hind legs for him to take holt of, which was his main dependence in a fight, and then he limped off a piece and laid down and died. It was a good pup, was that Andrew Jackson, and would have made a name for hisself if he'd lived, for the stuff was in him and he had genius — I know it, because he hadn't no opportunities to speak of, and it don't stand to reason that a dog could make such a fight as he could under them circumstances if he hadn't no talent. It always makes me feel sorry when I think of that last fight of his'n, and the way it turned out.

"Well, thish-yer Smiley had rat-tarriers, and chicken cocks, and tomcats and all them kind of things, till you couldn't rest, and you couldn't fetch nothing for him to bet on but he'd match you. He ketched a frog one day, and took him home, and said he cal'lated to educate him; and so he never done nothing for three months but set in his back yard and learn that frog to jump. And you bet you he *did* learn him, too. He'd give him a little punch behind, and the next minute you'd see that frog whirling in the air like a doughnut — see him turn one summerset, or maybe a couple, if he got a good start, and come down flat-footed and all right, like a cat. He got him up so in the matter of ketching flies, and kep' him in practice so constant, that he'd nail a fly every time as fur as he could see him. Smiley said all a frog wanted was education, and he could do 'most anything — and I believe him. Why, I've seen him set Dan'l Webster down here on this floor — Dan'l Webster was the name of the frog — and sing out, 'Flies, Dan'l, flies!' and quicker'n you could wink he'd spring straight up and snake a fly off'n the counter there, and flop down on the floor ag'in as solid as a gob of mud, and fall to scratching the side of his head with his hind foot as indifferent as if he hadn't no idea he'd been doin' any more'n any frog might do. You never see a frog so modest and straightfor'ard as he was, for all he was so gifted. And when it come to fair and square jumping on a dead level, he could get over more ground at one straddle than any animal of his breed you ever see. Jumping on a dead level was his strong suit, you understand; and when it come to that, Smiley would ante up money on him as long as he had a red. Smiley was monstrous proud of his frog, and well he might be, for fellers that had traveled and been everywheres all said he laid over any frog that ever *they* see.

"Well, Smiley kep' the beast in a little lattice box, and he used to fetch him down-town sometimes and lay for a bet. One day a feller — a stranger in the camp, he was — come acrost him with his box, and says:

" 'What might it be that you've got in the box?'

"And Smiley says, sorter indifferent-like, 'It might be a parrot, or it might be a canary, maybe, but it ain't — it's only just a frog.'

"And the feller took it, and looked at it careful, and turned it round this way and that, and says, 'H'm — so 'tis. Well, what's *he* good for?'

" 'Well,' Smiley says, easy and careless, 'he's good enough for *one* thing, I should judge — he can outjump any frog in Calaveras County.'

"The feller took the box again, and took another long, particular look, and give it back to Smiley, and says, very deliberate, 'Well,' he says, 'I don't see no p'ints about that frog that's any better'n any other frog.'

" 'Maybe you don't,' Smiley says. 'Maybe you understand frogs and maybe you don't understand 'em; maybe you've had experience, and maybe you ain't only a amature, as it were. Anyways, I've got *my* opinion, and I'll resk forty dollars that he can outjump any frog in Calaveras County.'

"And the feller studied a minute, and then says, kinder sad-like, 'Well, I'm only a stranger here, and I ain't got no frog; but if I had a frog, I'd bet you.'

"And then Smiley says, 'That's all right — that's all right — if you'll hold my box a minute, I'll go and get you a frog.' And so the feller took the box, and put up his forty dollars along with Smiley's, and set down to wait.

"So he set there a good while thinking and thinking to himself, and then he got the frog out and prized his mouth

open and took a teaspoon and filled him full of quail-shot
— filled him pretty near up to his chin — and set him on
the floor. Smiley he went to the swamp and slopped around
in the mud for a long time, and finally he ketched a frog,
and fetched him in, and give him to this feller, and says:

" 'Now, if you're ready, set him alongside of Dan'l, with
his fore paws just even with Dan'l's, and I'll give the word.'
Then he says, 'One — two — three — *git!* and him and
the feller touched up the frogs from behind, and the new
frog hopped off lively, but Dan'l give a heave, and hysted up
his shoulders — so — like a Frenchman, but it warn't no
use — he couldn't budge; he was planted as solid as a
church, and he couldn't no more stir than if he was an-
chored out. Smiley was a good deal surprised, and he was
disgusted too, but he didn't have no idea what the matter
was, of course.

"The feller took the money and started away; and when
he was going out at the door, he sorter jerked his thumb
over his shoulder — so — at Dan'l, and says again, very deliberate, 'Well,' he says, 'I don't see no p'ints about that frog
that's any better'n any other frog.'

"Smiley he stood scratching his head and looking down
at Dan'l a long time, and at last he says, 'I do wonder what
in the nation that frog throw'd off for — I wonder if there
ain't something the matter with him — he 'pears to look
mighty baggy, somehow.' And he ketched Dan'l by the nap
of the neck, and hefted him, and says, 'Why blame my
cats if he don't weigh five pound!' and turned him upside
down and he belched out a double handful of shot. And
then he see how it was, and he was the maddest man — he
set the frog down and took out after the feller, but he never
ketched him. And — "

[Here Simon Wheeler heard his name called from the
front yard, and got up to see what was wanted.] And turn-

ing to me as he moved away, he said: "Just set where you are, stranger, and rest easy — I ain't going to be gone a second."

But, by your leave, I did not think that a continuation of the history of the enterprising vagabond *Jim* Smiley would be likely to afford me much information concerning the Rev. *Leonidas W.* Smiley, and so I started away.

At the door I met the sociable Wheeler returning, and he buttonholed me and recommenced:

"Well, thish-yer Smiley had a yaller one-eyed cow that didn't have no tail, only just a short stump like a bannanner, and — "

However, lacking both time and inclination, I did not wait to hear about the afflicted cow, but took my leave.

THE STORY OF THE BAD LITTLE BOY

Once there was a bad little boy whose name was Jim — though, if you will notice, you will find that bad little boys are nearly always called James in your Sunday-school books. It was strange, but still it was true, that this one was called Jim.

He didn't have any sick mother, either — a sick mother who was pious and had the consumption, and would be glad to lie down in the grave and be at rest but for the strong love she bore her boy, and the anxiety she felt that the world might be harsh and cold toward him when she was gone. Most bad boys in the Sunday books are named James, and have sick mothers, who teach them to say, "Now, I lay me down," etc., and sing them to sleep with sweet, plaintive voices, and then kiss them good night, and kneel down by the bedside and weep. But it was different with this fellow. He was named Jim, and there wasn't anything the matter with his mother — no consumption, nor anything of that kind. She was rather stout than otherwise, and she was not pious; moreover, she was not anxious on Jim's account. She said if he were to break his neck it wouldn't be much loss. She always spanked Jim to sleep, and she never kissed him good night; on the contrary, she boxed his ears when she was ready to leave him.

Once this little bad boy stole the key of the pantry, and slipped in there and helped himself to some jam, and filled up the vessel with tar, so that his mother would never know the difference; but all at once a terrible feeling didn't come over him, and something didn't seem to whisper to him, "Is it right to disobey my mother? Isn't it sinful to do this? Where do bad little boys go who gobble up their good kind mother's jam?" and then he didn't kneel down all alone and promise never to be wicked any more, and rise up with a light, happy heart, and go and tell his mother all about it, and beg her forgiveness, and be blessed by her with tears of pride and thankfulness in her eyes. No; that is the way with all other bad boys in the books; but it happened otherwise with this Jim, strangely enough. He ate that jam, and said it was bully, in his sinful, vulgar way; and he put in the tar, and said that was bully also, and laughed, and observed "that the old woman would get up and snort" when she found it out; and when she did find it out, he denied knowing anything about it, and she whipped him severely, and he did the crying himself. Everything about this boy was curious — everything turned out differently with him from the way it does to the bad Jameses in the books.

Once he climbed up in Farmer Acorn's apple trees to steal apples, and the limb didn't break, and he didn't fall and break his arm, and get torn by the farmer's great dog, and then languish on a sickbed for weeks, and repent and become good. Oh, no; he stole as many apples as he wanted and came down all right; and he was all ready for the dog, too, and knocked him endways with a brick when he came to tear him. It was very strange — nothing like it ever happened in those mild little books with marbled backs, and with pictures in them of men with swallow-tailed coats and bell-crowned hats, and pantaloons that are short in the legs, and women with the waists of their dresses under their arms, and no hoops on. Nothing like it in any of the Sunday-school books.

Once he stole the teacher's penknife, and, when he was afraid it would be found out and he would get whipped, he slipped it into George Wilson's cap — poor Widow Wilson's son, the moral boy, the good little boy of the village, who always obeyed his mother, and never told an untruth, and was fond of his lessons, and infatuated with Sunday-School. And when the knife dropped from the cap, and poor George hung his head and blushed, as if in conscious guilt, and the grieved teacher charged the theft upon him, and was just in the very act of bringing the switch down upon his trembling shoulders, a white-haired, improbable justice of the peace did not suddenly appear in their midst, and strike an attitude and say, "Spare this noble boy — there stands the cowering culprit! I was passing the school door at recess, and, unseen myself, I saw the theft committed!" And then Jim didn't get whaled, and the venerable justice didn't read the tearful school a homily, and take George by the hand and say such a boy deserved to be exalted, and then tell him to come and make his home with him, and sweep out the office, and make fires, and run errands, and chop wood, and study law, and help his wife do household labors, and have all the balance of the time to play, and get forty cents a month, and be happy. No; it would have happened that way in the books, but it didn't happen that way to Jim. No meddling old clam of a justice dropped in to make trouble, and so the model boy George got thrashed, and Jim was glad of it because, you know, Jim hated moral boys. Jim said he was "down on them milksops." Such was the coarse language of this bad, neglected boy.

But the strangest thing that ever happened to Jim was the
time he went boating on Sunday, and didn't get drowned,
and that other time that he got caught out in the storm
when he was fishing on Sunday, and didn't get struck by
lightning. Why, you might look, and look, all through the
Sunday-school books from now till next Christmas, and
you would never come across anything like this. Oh, no;
you would find that all the bad boys who go boating on
Sunday invariably get drowned; and all the bad boys who
get caught out in storms when they are fishing on Sunday
infallibly get struck by lightning. Boats with bad boys in
them always upset on Sunday, and it always storms when
bad boys go fishing on the Sabbath. How this Jim ever escaped is a mystery to me.

This Jim bore a charmed life — that must have been the
way of it. Nothing could hurt him. He even gave the elephant in the menagerie a plug of tobacco, and the elephant
didn't knock the top of his head off with his trunk. He
browsed around the cupboard after essence of peppermint,
and didn't make a mistake and drink *aqua fortis*. He stole
his father's gun and went hunting on the Sabbath, and
didn't shoot three or four of his fingers off. He struck his little sister on the temple with his fist when he was angry, and
she didn't linger in pain through long summer days, and die
with sweet words of forgiveness upon her lips that redou-
bled the anguish of his breaking heart. No; she got over it.
He ran off and went to sea at last, and didn't come back and
find himself sad and alone in the world, his loved ones
sleeping in the quiet churchyard, and the vine-embowered
home of his boyhood tumbled down and gone to decay. Ah,
no; he came home as drunk as a piper, and got into the
station-house the first thing.

And he grew up and married, and raised a large family,
and brained them all with an ax one night, and got wealthy

by all manner of cheating and rascality; and now he is the infernalest wickedest scoundrel in his native village, and is universally respected, and belongs to the legislature.

So you see there never was a bad James in the Sunday-school books that had such a streak of luck as this sinful Jim with the charmed life.

Is He Living or
Is He Dead?

I was spending the month of March, 1892, at Mentone, in the Riviera. At this retired spot one has all the advantages, privately, which are to be had at Monte Carlo and Nice, a few miles farther along, publicly. That is to say, one has the flooding sunshine, the balmy air, and the brilliant blue sea, without the marring additions of human powwow and fuss and feathers and display. Mentone is quiet, simple, restful, unpretentious; the rich and the gaudy do not come there. As a rule, I mean, the rich do not come there. Now and then a rich man comes, and I presently got acquainted with one of these. Partially to disguise him I will call him Smith. One day, in the Hôtel des Anglais, at the second breakfast, he exclaimed:

"Quick! Cast your eye on the man going out at the door. Take in every detail of him."

"Why?"

"Do you know who he is?"

"Yes. He spent several days here before you came. He is an old, retired, and very rich silk manufacturer from Lyons, they say, and I guess he is alone in the world, for he always looks sad and dreamy, and doesn't talk with anybody. His name is Theóphile Magnan."

I supposed that Smith would now proceed to justify the

large interest which he had shown in Monsieur Magnan; but instead he dropped into a brown study, and was apparently lost to me and to the rest of the world during some minutes. Now and then he passed his fingers through his flossy white hair, to assist his thinking, and meantime he allowed his breakfast to go on cooling. At last he said:

"No, it's gone; I can't call it back."

"Can't call what back?"

"It's one of Hans Andersen's beautiful little stories. But it's gone from me. Part of it is like this: A child has a caged bird, which it loves, but thoughtlessly neglects. The bird pours out its song unheard and unheeded; but in time, hunger and thirst assail the creature, and its song grows plaintive and feeble and finally ceases — the bird dies. The child comes, and is smitten to the heart with remorse; then, with bitter tears and lamentations, it calls its mates, and they bury the bird with elaborate pomp and the tenderest grief, without knowing, poor things, that it isn't children only who starve poets to death and then spend enough on their funerals and monuments to have kept them alive and made them easy and comfortable. Now — "

But here we were interrupted. About ten that evening I ran across Smith, and he asked me up to his parlor to help him smoke and drink hot Scotch. It was a cozy place, with its comfortable chairs, its cheerful lamps, and its friendly open fire of seasoned olive-wood. To make everything perfect, there was the muffled booming of the surf outside. After the second Scotch and much lazy and contented chat, Smith said:

"Now we are properly primed — I to tell a curious history, and you to listen to it. It has been a secret for many years — a secret between me and three others; but I am going to break the seal now. Are you comfortable?"

"Perfectly. Go on."
Here follows what he told me:

A long time ago I was a young artist — a very young
artist, in fact — and I wandered about the country parts of
France, sketching here and sketching there, and was
presently joined by a couple of darling young Frenchmen
who were at the same kind of thing that I was doing. We
were as happy as we were poor, or as poor as we were
happy — phrase it to suit yourself. Claude Frère and Carl
Boulanger — these are the names of those boys; dear, dear
fellows, and the sunniest spirits that ever laughed at poverty
and had a noble good time in all weathers.

At last we ran hard aground in a Breton village, and an
artist as poor as ourselves took us in and literally saved us
from starving — François Millet —

"What! the *great* François Millet?"

Great? He wasn't any greater than we were, then. He
hadn't any fame, even in his own village; and he was so
poor that he hadn't anything to feed us on but turnips, and
even the turnips failed us sometimes. We four became fast
friends, doting friends, inseparables. We painted away together with all our might, piling up stock, piling up stock,
but very seldom getting rid of any of it. We had lovely times
together; but, O my soul! how we were pinched now and
then!

For a little over two years this went on. At last, one day,
Claude said:

"Boys, we've come to the end. Do you understand that?
— absolutely to the end. Everybody has struck — there's a
league formed against us. I've been all around the village
and it's just as I tell you. They refuse to credit us for another
centime until all the odds and ends are paid up."

This struck us cold. Every face was blank with dismay.

We realized that our circumstances were desperate, now. There was a long silence. Finally, Millet said with a sigh:

"Nothing occurs to me — nothing. Suggest something, lads."

There was no response, unless a mournful silence may be called a response. Carl got up, and walked nervously up and down awhile, then said:

"It's a shame! Look at these canvases: stacks and stacks of as good pictures as anybody in Europe paints — I don't care who he is. Yes, and plenty of lounging strangers have said the same — or nearly that, anyway."

"But didn't buy," Millet said.

"No matter, they said it; and it's true, too. Look at your 'Angelus' there! Will anybody tell me — "

"Pah, Carl — my 'Angelus'! I was offered five francs for it."

"When?"

"Who offered it?"

"Where is he?"

"Why didn't you take it?"

"Come — don't all speak at once. I thought he would give more — I was sure of it — he looked it — so I asked him eight."

"Well — and then?"

"He said he would call again."

"Thunder and lightning! Why, François — "

"Oh, I know — I know! It was a mistake, and I was a fool. Boys, I meant for the best; you'll grant me that, and I — "

"Why, certainly, we know that, bless your dear heart; but don't you be a fool again."

"I? I wish somebody would come along and offer us a cabbage for it — you'd see!"

"A cabbage! Oh, don't name it — it makes my mouth water. Talk of things less trying."

"Boys," said Carl, "*do* these pictures lack merit? Answer me that."

"No!"

"Aren't they of very great and high merit? Answer me that."

"Yes."

"Of such great and high merit that, if an illustrious name were attached to them, they would sell at splendid prices. Isn't it so?"

"Certainly it is. Nobody doubts that."

"But — I'm not joking — *isn't* it so?"

"Why, of course it's so — and *we* are not joking. But what of it? What of it? How does that concern us?"

"In this way, comrades — we'll *attach* an illustrious name to them!"

The lively conversation stopped. The faces were turned inquiringly upon Carl. What sort of riddle might this be? Where was an illustrious name to be borrowed? And who was to borrow it?

Carl sat down, and said:

"Now, I have a perfectly serious thing to propose. I think it is the only way to keep us out of the almshouse, and I believe it to be a perfectly sure way. I base this opinion upon certain multitudinous and long-established facts in human history. I believe my project will make us all rich."

"Rich! You've lost your mind."

"No, I haven't."

"Yes, you have — you've lost your mind. What do you *call* rich?"

"A hundred thousand francs apiece."

"He *has* lost his mind. I knew it."

"Yes, he has. Carl, privation has been too much for you, and — "

"Carl, you want to take a pill and get right to bed."

"Bandage him first — bandage his head, and then — "

"No, bandage his heels; his brains have been settling for weeks — I've noticed it."

"Shut up!" said Millet, with ostensible severity, "and let the boy say his say. Now, then — come out with your project, Carl. What is it?"

"Well, then, by way of preamble I will ask you to note this fact in human history: that the merit of many a great artist has never been acknowledged until after he was starved and dead. This has happened so often that I make bold to found a law upon it. This law: that the merit of *every* great unknown and neglected artist must and will be recognized, and his pictures climb to high prices after his death. My project is this: we must cast lots — one of us must die."

The remark fell so calmly and so unexpectedly that we almost forgot to jump. Then there was a wild chorus of advice again — medical advice — for the help of Carl's brain; but he waited patiently for the hilarity to calm down, then went on again with his project.

"Yes, one of us must die, to save the others — and himself. We will cast lots. The one chosen shall be illustrious, all of us shall be rich. Hold still, now — hold still; don't interrupt — I tell you I know what I am talking about. Here is the idea. During the next three months the one who is to die shall paint with all his might, enlarge his stock all he can — not pictures, *no!* skeleton sketches, studies, parts of studies, fragments of studies, a dozen dabs of the brush on each — meaningless, of course, but *his* with his cipher on them; turn out fifty a day, each to contain some peculiarity or

mannerism, easily detectable as his — *they're* the things that
sell you know, and are collected at fabulous prices for the
world's museums, after the great man is gone; we'll have a
ton of them ready — a ton! And all that time the rest of us
will be busy supporting the moribund, and working Paris
and the dealers — preparations for the coming event, you
know; and when everything is hot and just right, we'll
spring the death on them and have the notorious funeral.
You get the idea?"

"N-o; at least, not qu — "

"Not quite? Don't you see? The man doesn't really die; he
changes his name and vanishes; we bury a dummy, and cry
over it, with all the world to help. And I — "

But he wasn't allowed to finish. Everybody broke out
into a rousing hurrah of applause; and all jumped up and
capered about the room and fell on each other's necks in
transports of gratitude and joy. For hours we talked over the
great plan, without ever feeling hungry; and at last, when all
the details had been arranged satisfactorily, we cast lots and
Millet was elected — elected to die, as we called it. Then we
scraped together those things which one never parts with
until he is betting them against future wealth — keepsake
trinkets and such like — and these we pawned for enough
to furnish us a frugal farewell supper and breakfast, and
leave us a few francs over for travel, and a stake of turnips
and such for Millet to live on for a few days.

Next morning, early, the three of us cleared out, straightway after breakfast — on foot, of course. Each of us carried
a dozen of Millet's small pictures, purposing to market
them. Carl struck for Paris, where he would start the work
of building up Millet's fame against the coming great day.
Claude and I were to separate, and scatter abroad over
France.

Now, it will surprise you to know what an easy and comfortable thing we had. I walked two days before I began business. Then I began to sketch a villa in the outskirts of a big town — because I saw the proprietor standing on an upper veranda. He came down to look on — I thought he would. I worked swiftly, intending to keep him interested. Occasionally he fired off a little ejaculation of approbation, and by and by he spoke up with enthusiasm, and said I was a master!

I put down my brush, reached into my satchel, fetched out a Millet, and pointed to the cipher in the corner. I said, proudly:

"I suppose you recognize *that*? Well, he taught me! I should *think* I ought to know my trade!"

The man looked guiltily embarrassed, and was silent. I said, sorrowfully:

"You don't mean to intimate that you don't know the cipher of François Millet!"

Of course he didn't know that cipher; but he was the gratefulest man you ever saw, just the same, for being let out of an uncomfortable place on such easy terms. He said:

"No! Why, it *is* Millet's, sure enough! I don't know what I could have been thinking of. Of course I recognize it now."

Next, he wanted to buy it; but I said that although I wasn't rich I wasn't *that* poor. However, at last, I let him have it for eight hundred francs.

"Eight hundred!"

Yes. Millet would have sold it for a pork-chop. Yes, I got eight hundred francs for that little thing. I wish I could get it back for eighty thousand. But that time's gone by. I made a very nice picture of that man's house, and I wanted to offer it to him for ten francs, but that wouldn't answer, seeing I was the pupil of such a master, so I sold it to him for a hundred. I sent the eight hundred francs straight back to Millet from that town and struck out again next day.

But I didn't walk — no. I rode. I have ridden ever since. I sold one picture every day, and never tried to sell two. I always said to my customer:

"I am a fool to sell a picture of François Millet's at all, for that man is not going to live three months, and when he dies his pictures can't be had for love or money."

I took care to spread that little fact as far as I could, and prepare the world for the event.

I take credit to myself for our plan of selling the pictures — it was mine. I suggested it that last evening when we were laying out our campaign, and all three of us agreed to give it a good fair trial before giving it up for some other. It succeeded with all of us. I walked only two days, Claude walked two — both of us afraid to make Millet celebrated too close to home — but Carl walked only half a day, the bright, conscienceless rascal, and after that he traveled like a duke.

Every now and then we got in with a country editor and started an item around through the press; not an item announcing that a new painter had been discovered, but an item which let on that everybody knew François Millet; not an item praising him in any way, but merely a word concerning the present condition of the "master" — sometimes hopeful, sometimes despondent, but always tinged with fears for the worst. We always marked these paragraphs, and sent the papers to all the people who had bought pictures of us.

Carl was soon in Paris, and he worked things with a high hand. He made friends with the correspondents, and got Millet's condition reported to England and all over the continent, and America, and everywhere.

At the end of six weeks from the start, we three met in

Paris and called a halt, and stopped sending back to Millet for additional pictures. The boom was so high, and everything so ripe, that we saw that it would be a mistake not to strike now, right away, without waiting any longer. So we wrote Millet to go to bed and begin to waste away pretty fast, for we should like him to die in ten days if he could get ready.

Then we figured up and found that among us we had sold eighty-five small pictures and studies, and had sixty-nine thousand francs to show for it. Carl had made the last sale and the most brilliant one of all. He sold the "Angelus" for twenty-two hundred francs. How we did glorify him! — not foreseeing that a day was coming by and by when France would struggle to own it and a stranger would capture it for five hundred and fifty thousand, cash.

We had a wind-up champagne supper that night, and next day Claude and I packed up and went off to nurse Millet through his last days and keep busybodies out of the house and send daily bulletins to Carl in Paris for publication in the papers of several continents for the information of a waiting world. The sad end came at last, and Carl was there in time to help in the final mournful rites.

You remember that great funeral, and what a stir it made all over the globe, and how the illustrious of two worlds came to attend it and testify their sorrow. We four — still inseparable — carried the coffin, and would allow none to help. And we were right about that, because it hadn't anything in it but a wax figure, and any other coffin-bearers would have found fault with the weight. Yes, we same old four, who had lovingly shared privation together in the old hard times now gone forever, carried the cof —

"Which four?"

"*We* four — for Millet helped to carry his own coffin. In

disguise, you know. Disguised as a relative — distant relative."

"Astonishing!"

"But true, just the same. Well, you remember how the pictures went up. Money? We didn't know what to do with it. There's a man in Paris to-day who owns seventy Millet pictures. He paid us two million francs for them. And as for the bushels of sketches and studies which Millet shoveled out during the six weeks that we were on the road, well, it would astonish you to know the figure we sell them at nowadays — that is, when we consent to let one go!"

"It is a wonderful history, perfectly wonderful!"

"Yes — it amounts to that."

"Whatever became of Millet?"

"Can you keep a secret?"

"I can."

"Do you remember the man I called your attention to in the dining-room to-day? *That was François Millet.*"

"Great — "

"Scott! Yes. For once they didn't starve a genius to death and then put into other pockets the rewards he should have had himself. *This* songbird was not allowed to pipe out its heart unheard and then be paid with the cold pomp of a big funeral. We looked out for that."

THE MAN THAT CORRUPTED HADLEYBURG

1

It was many years ago. Hadleyburg was the most honest and upright town in all the region around about. It had kept that reputation unsmirched during three generations, and was prouder of it than of any other of its possessions. It was so proud of it, and so anxious to insure its perpetuation, that it began to teach the principles of honest dealing to its babies in the cradle, and made the like teachings the staple of their culture thenceforward through all the years devoted to their education. Also, throughout the formative years temptations were kept out of the way of the young people, so that their honesty could have every chance to harden and solidify, and become a part of their very bone. The neighboring towns were jealous of this honorable supremacy, and affected to sneer at Hadleyburg's pride in it and call it vanity; but all the same they were obliged to acknowledge that Hadleyburg was in reality an incorruptible town; and if pressed they would also acknowledge that the mere fact that a young man hailed from Hadleyburg was all the recommendation he needed when he went forth from his natal town to seek for responsible employment.

But at last, in the drift of time, Hadleyburg had the ill luck to offend a passing stranger — possibly without know-

ing it, certainly without caring, for Hadleyburg was suffi-
cient unto itself, and cared not a rap for strangers or their
opinions. Still, it would have been well to make an excep-
tion in this one's case, for he was a bitter man and revenge-
ful. All through his wanderings during a whole year he kept
his injury in mind, and gave all his leisure moments to trying to invent a compensating satisfaction for it. He con-
trived many plans, and all of them were good, but none of
them was quite sweeping enough; the poorest of them
would hurt a great many individuals, but what he wanted
was a plan which would comprehend the entire town, and
not let so much as one person escape unhurt. At last he had
a fortunate idea, and when it fell into his brain it lit up his
whole head with an evil joy. He began to form a plan at
once, saying to himself, "That is the thing to do — I will
corrupt the town."

Six months later he went to Hadleyburg, and arrived in
a buggy at the house of the old cashier of the bank about
ten at night. He got a sack out of the buggy, shouldered it,
and staggered with it through the cottage yard, and
knocked at the door. A woman's voice said "Come in," and
he entered, and set his sack behind the stove in the parlor,
saying politely to the old lady who sat reading the *Mission-
ary Herald* by the lamp:

"Pray keep your seat, madam, I will not disturb you.
There — now it is pretty well concealed; one would hardly
know it was there. Can I see your husband a moment,
madam?"

No, he was gone to Brixton, and might not return before
morning.

"Very well, madam, it is no matter. I merely wanted to
leave that sack in his care, to be delivered to the rightful
owner when he shall be found. I am a stranger; he does not
know me; I am merely passing through the town to-night

to discharge a matter which has been long in my mind. My errand is now completed, and I go pleased and a little proud, and you will never see me again. There is a paper attached to the sack which will explain everything. Good night, madam."

The old lady was afraid of the mysterious big stranger, and was glad to see him go. But her curiosity was roused, and she went straight to the sack and brought away the paper. It began as follows:

TO BE PUBLISHED; *or, the right man sought out by private inquiry — either will answer. This sack contains gold coin weighing a hundred and sixty pounds four ounces —*

"Mercy on us, and the door not locked!"

Mrs. Richards flew to it all in a tremble and locked it, then pulled down the window-shades and stood frightened, worried, and wondering if there was anything else she could do toward making herself and the money more safe. She listened awhile for burglars, then surrendered to curiosity and went back to the lamp and finished reading the paper:

I am a foreigner, and am presently going back to my own country, to remain there permanently. I am grateful to America for what I have received at her hands during my long stay under her flag; and to one of her citizens — a citizen of Hadleyburg — I am especially grateful for a great kindness done me a year or two ago. Two great kindnesses, in fact. I will explain. I was a gambler. I say I WAS. I was a ruined gambler. I arrived in this village at night, hungry and without a penny. I asked for help — in the dark; I was ashamed to beg in the light. I begged of the right man. He gave me twenty dollars — that is to say, he gave me life, as I considered it. He also gave me fortune; for out of that money I have made myself rich at the gaming-table. And finally, a remark which he made to me has remained with me to this day, and has at last conquered me; and in conquering has saved the remnant of my morals; I shall gamble no more. Now I have no idea who that man was, but I want him found, and I want him to have this money, to give away, throw away, or keep, as he pleases. It is merely my way of testifying my gratitude to him. If I could stay, I would find him myself; but no matter, he will be found. This is an honest town, an incorruptible town, and I know I can trust it without fear. This man can be identified by the remark which he made to me; I feel persuaded that he will remember it.

And now my plan is this: If you prefer to conduct the inquiry privately, do so. Tell the contents of this present writing to any one who is likely to be the right man. If he shall answer, 'I am the man; the remark I made was so-and-so,' apply the test — to wit: open the sack, and in it you will find a sealed envelope containing that remark. If the remark mentioned by the candidate tallies with it, give him the money, and ask no further questions, for he is certainly the right man.

But if you shall prefer a public inquiry, then publish this present writing in the local paper — with these instructions added, to wit: Thirty days from now, let the candidate appear at the town-hall at eight in the evening (Friday), and hand his remark, in a sealed envelope, to the Rev. Mr. Burgess (if he will be kind enough to act); and let Mr. Burgess there and then destroy the seals of the sack, open it, and see if the remark is correct; if correct, let the money be delivered with my sincere gratitude, to my benefactor thus identified.

Mrs. Richards sat down, gently quivering with excitement, and was soon lost in thinkings — after this pattern: "What a strange thing it is! . . . And what a fortune for that kind man who set his bread afloat upon the waters! . . . If it had only been my husband that did it! — for we are so poor, so old and poor! . . ." Then, with a sigh — "But it was not my Edward; no, it was not he that gave a stranger twenty dollars. It is pity, too; I see it now. . . ." Then, with a shudder — "But it is *gambler's* money! the wages of sin: we couldn't take it; we couldn't touch it. I don't like to be near it; it seems a defilement." She moved to a farther chair. . . . "I wish Edward would come and take it to the bank; a burglar might come at any moment; it is dreadful to be here all alone with it."

At eleven Mr. Richards arrived, and while his wife was saying, "I am *so* glad you've come!" he was saying, "I'm so tired — tired clear out; it is dreadful to be poor, and have to make these dismal journeys at my time of life. Always at the grind, grind, grind, on a salary — another man's slave, and he sitting at home in his slippers, rich and comfortable."

"I am so sorry for you, Edward, you know that; but be comforted: we have our livelihood; we have our good name — "

"Yes, Mary, and that is everything. Don't mind my talk — it's just a moment's irritation and doesn't mean anything. Kiss me — there, it's all gone now, and I am not complaining any more. What have you been getting? What's in the sack?"

Then his wife told him the great secret. It dazed him for a moment; then he said:

"It weighs a hundred and sixty pounds? Why, Mary, it's for-ty thousand dollars — think of it — a whole fortune! Not ten men in this village are worth that much. Give me the paper."

He skimmed through it and said:

"Isn't it an adventure! Why, it's a romance; it's like the impossible things one reads about in books, and never sees in life." He was well stirred up now; cheerful, even gleeful.

He tapped his old wife on the cheek, and said, humorously, "Why, we're rich, Mary, rich; all we've got to do is to bury the money and burn the papers. If the gambler ever comes to inquire, we'll merely look coldly upon him and say: 'What is this nonsense you are talking! We have never heard of you and your sack of gold before'; and then he would look foolish, and — "

"And in the mean time, while you are running on with your jokes, the money is still here, and it is fast getting along toward burglar-time."

"True. Very well, what shall we do — make the inquiry private? No, not that; it would spoil the romance. The public method is better. Think what a noise it will make! And it will make all the other towns jealous; for no stranger would trust such a thing to any town but Hadleyburg, and they know it. It's a great card for us. I must get to the printing-office now, or I shall be too late."

"But stop — stop — don't leave me here alone with it, Edward!"

But he was gone. For only a little while, however. Not far from his own house he met the editor-proprietor of the paper, and gave him the document, and said, "Here is a good thing for you, Cox — put it in."

"It may be too late, Mr. Richards, but I'll see."

At home again he and his wife sat down to talk the charming mystery over; they were in no condition for sleep. The first question was, Who could the citizen have been who gave the stranger the twenty dollars? It seemed a simple one; both answered it in the same breath:

"Barclay Goodson."

"Yes," said Richards, "he could have done it, and it would have been like him, but there's not another in the town."

"Everybody will grant that, Edward — grant it privately,

anyway. For six months, now, the village has been its own proper self once more — honest, narrow, self-righteous, and stingy."

"It is what he always called it, to the day of his death — said it right out publicly, too."

"Yes, and he was hated for it."

"Oh, of course; but he didn't care. I reckon he was the best-hated man among us, except the Reverend Burgess."

"Well, Burgess deserves it — he will never get another congregation here. Mean as the town is, it knows how to estimate *him*. Edward, doesn't it seem odd that the stranger should appoint Burgess to deliver the money?"

"Well, yes — it does. That is — that is — "

"Why so much that-*is*-ing? Would *you* select him?"

"Mary, maybe the stranger knows him better than this village does."

"Much *that* would help Burgess!"

The husband seemed perplexed for an answer; the wife kept a steady eye upon him, and waited. Finally Richards said, with the hesitancy of one who is making a statement which is likely to encounter doubt:

"Mary, Burgess is not a bad man."

His wife was certainly surprised.

"Nonsense!" she exclaimed.

"He is not a bad man. I know. The whole of his unpopularity had its foundation in that one thing — the thing that made so much noise."

"That 'one thing,' indeed! As if that 'one thing' wasn't enough, all by itself."

"Plenty. Plenty. Only he wasn't guilty of it."

"How you talk! Not guilty of it! Everybody knows he *was* guilty."

"Mary, I give you my word — he was innocent."

"I can't believe it, and I don't. How do you know?"

"It is a confession. I am ashamed, but I will make it. I was the only man who knew he was innocent. I could have saved him, and — and — well, you know how the town was wrought up — I hadn't the pluck to do it. It would have turned everybody against me. I felt mean, ever so mean; but I didn't dare; I hadn't the manliness to face that."

Mary looked troubled, and for a while was silent. Then she said, stammeringly:

"I — I don't think it would have done for you to — to — One mustn't — er — public opinion — one has to be so careful — so — " It was a difficult road, and she got mired; but after a little she got started again. "It was a great pity, but — Why, we couldn't afford it, Edward — we couldn't indeed. Oh, I wouldn't have had you do it for anything!"

"It would have lost us the good will of so many people, Mary; and then — and then — "

"What troubles me now is, what *he* thinks of us, Edward."

"He? *He* doesn't suspect that I could have saved him."

"Oh," exclaimed the wife, in a tone of relief, "I am glad of that! As long as he doesn't know that you could have saved him, he — he — well, that makes it a great deal better. Why, I might have known he didn't know, because he is always trying to be friendly with us, as little encouragement as we give him. More than once people have twitted me with it. There's the Wilsons, and the Wilcoxes, and the Harknesses, they take a mean pleasure in saying, '*Your friend* Burgess,' because they know it pesters me. I wish he wouldn't persist in liking us so; I can't think why he keeps it up."

"I can explain it. It's another confession. When the thing was new and hot, and the town made a plan to ride him on a rail, my conscience hurt me so that I couldn't stand it, and

I went privately and gave him notice, and he got out of the town and staid out till it was safe to come back."

"Edward! If the town had found it out — "

"*Don't!* It scares me yet, to think of it. I repented of it the minute it was done; and I was even afraid to tell you, lest your face might betray it to somebody. I didn't sleep any that night, for worrying. But after a few days I saw that no one was going to suspect me, and after that I got to feeling glad I did it. And I feel glad yet, Mary — glad through and through."

"So do I, now, for it would have been a dreadful way to treat him. Yes, I'm glad; for really you did owe him that, you know. But, Edward, suppose it should come out yet, some day!"

"It won't."

"Why?"

"Because everybody thinks it was Goodson."

"Of course they would!"

"Certainly. And of course *he* didn't care. They persuaded poor old Sawlsberry to go and charge it on him, and he went blustering over there and did it. Goodson looked him over, like as if he was hunting for a place on him that he could despise the most, then he says, 'So you are the Committee of Inquiry, are you?' Sawlsberry said that was about what he was. 'Hm. Do they require particulars, or do you reckon a kind of a *general* answer will do?' 'If they require particulars, I will come back, Mr. Goodson; I will take the general answer first.' 'Very well, then, tell them to go to hell — I reckon that's general enough. And I'll give you some advice, Sawlsberry; when you come back for the particulars, fetch a basket to carry the relics of yourself home in.' "

"Just like Goodson; it's got all the marks. He had only one vanity: he thought he could give advice better than any other person."

"It settled the business, and saved us, Mary. The subject was dropped."

"Bless you, I'm not doubting *that.*"

Then they took up the gold-sack mystery again, with strong interest. Soon the conversation began to suffer breaks — interruptions caused by absorbed thinkings. The breaks grew more and more frequent. At last Richards lost himself wholly in thought. He sat long, gazing vacantly at the floor, and by and by he began to punctuate his thoughts with little nervous movements of his hands that seemed to indicate vexation. Meantime his wife too had relapsed into a thoughtful silence, and her movements were beginning to show a troubled discomfort. Finally Richards got up and strode aimlessly about the room, plowing his hands through his hair, much as a somnambulist might do who was having a bad dream. Then he seemed to arrive at a definite purpose; and without a word he put on his hat and passed quickly out of the house. His wife sat brooding, with a drawn face, and did not seem to be aware that she was alone. Now and then she murmured, "Lead us not into t — . . . but — but — we are so poor, so poor! . . . Lead us not into . . . Ah, who would be hurt by it? — and no one would ever know. . . . Lead us . . ." The voice died out in mumblings. After a little she glanced up and muttered in a half-frightened, half-glad way:

"He is gone! But, oh dear, he may be too late — too late. . . . Maybe not — maybe there is still time." She rose and stood thinking, nervously clasping and unclasping her hands. A slight shudder shook her frame, and she said, out of a dry throat, "God forgive me — it's awful to think such things — but . . . Lord, how we are made — how strangely we are made!"

She turned the light low, and slipped stealthily over and knelt down by the sack and felt of its ridgy sides with her hands, and fondled them lovingly; and there was a gloating light in her poor old eyes. She fell into fits of absence; and came half out of them at times to mutter, "If we had only waited! — oh, if we had only waited a little, and not been in such a hurry!"

Meantime Cox had gone home from his office and told his wife all about the strange thing that had happened, and they had talked it over eagerly, and guessed that the late Goodson was the only man in the town who could have helped a suffering stranger with so noble a sum as twenty dollars. Then there was a pause, and the two became thoughtful and silent. And by and by nervous and fidgety. At last the wife said, as if to herself:

"Nobody knows this secret but the Richardses . . . and us . . . nobody."

The husband came out of his thinkings with a slight start, and gazed wistfully at his wife, whose face was become very pale; then he hesitatingly rose, and glanced furtively at his hat, then at his wife — a sort of mute inquiry. Mrs. Cox swallowed once or twice, with her hand at her throat, then in place of speech she nodded her head. In a moment she was alone, and mumbling to herself.

And now Richards and Cox were hurrying through the deserted streets, from opposite directions. They met, panting, at the foot of the printing-office stairs; by the night light there they read each other's face. Cox whispered:

"Nobody knows about this but us?"

The whispered answer was,

"Not a soul — on honor, not a soul!"

"If it isn't too late to — "

The men were starting up-stairs; at this moment they were overtaken by a boy, and Cox asked:

"Is that you, Johnny?"

"Yes, sir."

"You needn't ship the early mail — nor *any* mail; wait till I tell you."

"It's already gone, sir."

"*Gone?*" It had the sound of an unspeakable disappointment in it.

"Yes, sir. Time-table for Brixton and all the towns beyond changed to-day, sir — had to get the papers in twenty minutes earlier than common. I had to rush; if I had been two minutes later — "

The men turned and walked slowly away, not waiting to hear the rest. Neither of them spoke during ten minutes; then Cox said, in a vexed tone:

"What possessed you to be in such a hurry, *I* can't make out."

The answer was humble enough:

"I see it now, but somehow I never thought, you know, until it was too late. But the next time — "

"Next time be hanged! It won't come in a thousand years."

Then the friends separated without a good night, and dragged themselves home with the gait of mortally stricken men. At their homes their wives sprang up with an eager "Well?" — then saw the answer with their eyes and sank down sorrowing, without waiting for it to come in words. In both houses a discussion followed of a heated sort — a new thing; there had been discussions before, but not heated ones, not ungentle ones. The discussions to-night were a sort of seeming plagiarisms of each other. Mrs. Richards said,

"If you had only waited, Edward — if you had only stopped to think; but no, you must run straight to the printing-office and spread it all over the world."

"It *said* publish it."

"That is nothing; it also said do it privately, if you liked. There, now — is that true, or not?"

"Why, yes — yes, it is true; but when I thought what stir it would make, and what a compliment it was to Hadleyburg that a stranger should trust it so — "

"Oh, certainly, I know all that; but if you had only stopped to think, you would have seen that you *couldn't* find the right man, because he is in his grave, and hasn't left chick nor child nor relation behind him; and as long as the money went to somebody that awfully needed it, and nobody would be hurt by it, and — and — "

She broke down, crying. Her husband tried to think of some comforting thing to say, and presently came out with this:

"But after all, Mary, it must be for the best — it *must* be; we know that. And we must remember that it was so ordered — "

"Ordered! Oh, everything's *ordered*, when a person has to find some way out when he has been stupid. Just the same, it was *ordered* that the money should come to us in this special way, and it was you that must take it on yourself to go meddling with the designs of Providence — and who gave you the right? It was wicked, that is what it was — just blasphemous presumption, and no more becoming to a meek and humble professor of — "

"But, Mary, you know how we have been trained all our lives long, like the whole village, till it is absolutely second nature to us to stop not a single moment to think when there's an honest thing to be done — "

"Oh, I know it, I know it — it's been one everlasting training and training and training in honesty — honesty shielded, from the very cradle, against every possible temptation, and so it's *artificial* honesty, and weak as water when

temptation comes, as we have seen this night. God knows I
never had shade nor shadow of a doubt of my petrified and
indestructible honesty until now — and now, under the
very first big and real temptation, I — Edward, it is my be-
lief that this town's honesty is as rotten as mine is; as rotten
as yours is. It is a mean town, a hard, stingy town, and
hasn't a virtue in the world but this honesty it is so celebrated for and so conceited about; and so help me, I do believe that if ever the day comes that its honesty falls under
great temptation, its grand reputation will go to ruin like a
house of cards. There, now, I've made confession, and I feel
better; I am a humbug, and I've been one all my life, without knowing it. Let no man call me honest again — I will
not have it."

"I — well, Mary, I feel a good deal as you do; I certainly
do. It seems strange, too, so strange. I never could have believed it — never."

A long silence followed; both were sunk in thought. At
last the wife looked up and said:

"I know what you are thinking, Edward."

Richards had the embarrassed look of a person who is
caught.

"I am ashamed to confess it, Mary, but — "

"It's no matter, Edward, I was thinking the same question myself."

"I hope so. State it."

"You were thinking, if a body could only guess out *what
the remark was* that Goodson made to the stranger."

"It's perfectly true. I feel guilty and ashamed. And you?"

"I'm past it. Let us make a pallet here; we've got to stand
watch till the bank vault opens in the morning and admits
the sack. . . . Oh dear, oh dear — if we hadn't made the
mistake!"

The pallet was made, and Mary said:

"The open sesame — what could it have been? I do wonder what that remark could have been? But come; we will get to bed now."

"And sleep?"

"No: think."

"Yes, think."

By this time the Coxes too had completed their spat and their reconciliation, and were turning in — to think, to think, and toss, and fret, and worry over what the remark could possibly have been which Goodson made to the stranded derelict; that golden remark; that remark worth forty thousand dollars, cash.

The reason that the village telegraph-office was open later than usual that night was this: The foreman of Cox's paper was the local representative of the Associated Press. One might say its honorary representative, for it wasn't four times a year that he could furnish thirty words that would be accepted. But this time it was different. His despatch stating what he had caught got an instant answer:

Send the whole thing — all the details — twelve hundred words.

A colossal order! The foreman filled the bill; and he was the proudest man in the State. By breakfast-time the next morning the name of Hadleyburg the Incorruptible was on every lip in America, from Montreal to the Gulf, from the glaciers of Alaska to the orange-groves of Florida; and millions and millions of people were discussing the stranger and his money-sack, and wondering if the right man would be found, and hoping some more news about the matter would come soon — right away.

2

Hadleyburg village woke up world-celebrated — astonished — happy — vain. Vain beyond imagination. Its nineteen principal citizens and their wives went about shaking hands with each other, and beaming, and smiling, and congratulating, and saying *this* thing adds a new word to the dictionary — *Hadleyburg*, synonym for *incorruptible* — destined to live in dictionaries forever! And the minor and unimportant citizens and their wives went around acting in much the same way. Everybody ran to the bank to see the gold-sack; and before noon grieved and envious crowds began to flock in from Brixton and all neighboring towns; and that afternoon and next day reporters began to arrive from everywhere to verify the sack and its history and write the whole thing up anew, and make dashing free-hand pictures of the sack, and of Richards's house, and the bank, and the Presbyterian church, and the Baptist church, and the public square, and the town-hall where the test would be applied and the money delivered; and damnable portraits of the Richardses, and Pinkerton the banker, and Cox, and the foreman, and Reverend Burgess, and the postmaster — and even of Jack Halliday, who was the loafing, good-natured, no-account, irreverent fisherman, hunter, boys' friend, stray-dogs' friend, typical "Sam Lawson" of the town. The little mean, smirking, oily Pinkerton showed the sack to all comers, and rubbed his sleek palms together pleasantly, and enlarged upon the town's fine old reputation for honesty and upon this wonderful indorsement of it, and hoped and believed that the example would now spread far and wide over the American world, and be epoch-making in the matter of moral regeneration. And so on, and so on.

By the end of a week things had quieted down again; the wild intoxication of pride and joy had sobered to a soft sweet, silent delight — a sort of deep, nameless, unutterable content. All faces bore a look of peaceful, holy happiness.

Then a change came. It was a gradual change: so gradual that its beginnings were hardly noticed; maybe were not noticed at all, except by Jack Halliday, who always noticed everything; and always made fun of it, too, no matter what it was. He began to throw out chaffing remarks about people not looking quite so happy as they did a day or two ago; and next he claimed that the new aspect was deepening to positive sadness; next, that it was taking on a sick look; and finally he said that everybody was become so moody, thoughtful, and absentminded that he could rob the meanest man in town of a cent out of the bottom of his breeches pocket and not disturb his revery.

At this stage — or at about this stage — a saying like this was dropped at bedtime — with a sigh, usually — by the head of each of the nineteen principal households: "Ah, what *could* have been the remark that Goodson made?"

And straightway — with a shudder — came this, from the man's wife:

"Oh, *don't!* What horrible thing are you mulling in your mind? Put it away from you, for God's sake!"

But that question was wrung from those men again the next night — and got the same retort. But weaker.

And the third night the men uttered the question yet again — with anguish, and absently. This time — and the following night — the wives fidgeted feebly, and tried to say something. But didn't.

And the night after that they found their tongues and responded — longingly:

"Oh, if we *could* only guess!"

Halliday's comments grew daily more and more sparklingly disagreeable and disparaging. He went diligently about, laughing at the town, individually and in mass. But his laugh was the only one left in the village: it fell upon a hollow and mournful vacancy and emptiness. Not even a smile was findable anywhere. Halliday⁻ carried a cigar-box around on a tripod, playing that it was a camera, and halted all passers and aimed the thing and said, "Ready! — now look pleasant, please," but not even this capital joke could surprise the dreary faces into any softening.

So three weeks passed — one week was left. It was Saturday evening — after supper. Instead of the aforetime Saturday-evening flutter and bustle and shopping and larking, the streets were empty and desolate. Richards and his old wife sat apart in their little parlor — miserable and thinking. This was become their evening habit now: the lifelong habit which had preceded it, of reading, knitting, and contented chat, or receiving or paying neighborly calls, was dead and gone and forgotten, ages ago — two or three weeks ago; nobody talked now, nobody read, nobody visited — the whole village sat at home, sighing, worrying, silent. Trying to guess out that remark.

The postman left a letter. Richards glanced listlessly at the superscription and the postmark — unfamiliar, both — and tossed the letter on the table and resumed his might-have-beens and his hopeless dull miseries where he had left them off. Two or three hours later his wife got wearily up and was going away to bed without a good night — custom now — but she stopped near the letter and eyed it awhile with a dead interest, then broke it open, and began to skim it over. Richards, sitting there with his chair tilted back against the wall and his chin between his knees, heard something fall. It was his wife. He sprang to her side, but she cried out:

"Leave me alone, I am too happy. Read the letter — read it!"

He did. He devoured it, his brain reeling. The letter was from a distant state, and it said:

I am a stranger to you, but no matter: I have something to tell. I have just arrived home from Mexico, and learned about that episode. Of course you do not know who made that remark, but I know, and I am the only person living who does know. It was GOODSON. I knew him well, many years ago. I passed through your village that very night, and was his guest till the midnight train came along. I overheard him make that remark to the stranger in the dark — it was in Hale Alley. He and I talked of it the rest of the way home, and while smoking in his house. He mentioned many of your villagers in the course of his talk — most of them in a very uncomplimentary way, but two or three favorably; among these latter yourself. I say "favorably" — nothing stronger. I remember his saying he did not actually LIKE any person in the town — not one; but that you — I THINK he said you — am almost sure — had done him a very great service once, possibly without knowing the full value of it, and he wished he had a fortune, he would leave it to you when he died, and a curse apiece for the rest of the citizens. Now, then, if it was you that did him that service, you are his legitimate heir, and entitled to the sack of gold. I know that I can trust to your honor and honesty, for in a citizen of Hadleyburg these virtues are an unfailing inheritance, and so I am going to reveal to you the remark, well satisfied that if you are not the right man you will seek and find the right one and see that poor Goodson's debt of gratitude for the service referred to is paid. This is the remark: "YOU ARE FAR FROM BEING A BAD MAN: GO, AND REFORM."

HOWARD L. STEPHENSON

"Oh, Edward, the money is ours, and I am so grateful, *oh*, so grateful — kiss me, dear, it's forever since we kissed

— and we needed it so — the money — and now you are free of Pinkerton and his bank, and nobody's slave any more; it seems to me I could fly for joy."

It was a happy half-hour that the couple spent there on the settee caressing each other; it was the old days come again — days that had begun with their courtship and lasted without a break till the stranger brought the deadly money. By and by the wife said:

"Oh, Edward, how lucky it was you did him that grand service, poor Goodson! I never liked him, but I love him now. And it was fine and beautiful of you never to mention it or brag about it." Then, with a touch of reproach, "But you ought to have told *me*, Edward, you ought to have told your wife, you know."

"Well, I — er — well, Mary, you see — "

"Now stop hemming and hawing, and tell me about it, Edward. I always loved you, and now I'm proud of you. Everybody believes there was only one good generous soul in this village, and now it turns out that you — Edward, why don't you tell me?"

"Well — er — er — Why, Mary, I can't!"

"You *can't*? *Why* can't you?"

"You see, he — well, he — he made me promise I wouldn't."

The wife looked him over, and said, very slowly:

"Made — you — promise? Edward, what do you tell me that for?"

"Mary, do you think I would lie?"

She was troubled and silent for a moment, then she laid her hand within his and said:

"No . . . no. We have wandered far enough from our bearings — God spare us that! In all your life you have never uttered a lie. But now — now that the foundations of

things seem to be crumbling from under us, we — we — "
She lost her voice for a moment, then said, brokenly, "Lead
us not into temptation. . . . I think you made the promise,
Edward. Let it rest so. Let us keep away from that ground.
Now — that is all gone by; let us be happy again; it is no
time for clouds."

Edward found it something of an effort to comply, for
his mind kept wandering — trying to remember what the
service was that he had done Goodson.

The couple lay awake the most of the night, Mary happy
and busy, Edward busy but not so happy. Mary was planning what she would do with the money. Edward was trying to recall that service. At first his conscience was sore on
account of the lie he had told Mary — if it was a lie. After
much reflection — suppose it *was* a lie? What then? Was it
such a great matter? Aren't we always *acting* lies? Then why
not *tell* them? Look at Mary — look what she had done.
While he was hurrying off on his honest errand, what was
she doing? Lamenting because the papers hadn't been destroyed and the money kept! Is theft better than lying?

That point lost its sting — the lie dropped into the back-
ground and left comfort behind it. The next point came to
the front: *Had* he rendered that service? Well, here was
Goodson's own evidence as reported in Stephenson's letter;
there could be no better evidence than that — it was even
proof that he had rendered it. Of course. So that point was
settled. . . . No, not quite. He recalled with a wince that
this unknown Mr. Stephenson was just a trifle unsure as to
whether the performer of it was Richards or some other —
and, oh dear, he had put Richards on his honor! He must
himself decide whither that money must go — and Mr.
Stephenson was not doubting that if he was the wrong man
he would go honorably and find the right one. Oh, it was

odious to put a man in such a situation — ah, why couldn't Stephenson have left out that doubt! What did he want to intrude that for?

Further reflection. How did it happen that *Richards's* name remained in Stephenson's mind as indicating the right man, and not some other man's name? That looked good. Yes, that looked very good. In fact, it went on looking better and better, straight along — until by and by it grew into positive *proof.* And then Richards put the matter at once out of his mind, for he had a private instinct that a proof once established is better left so.

He was feeling reasonably comfortable now, but there was still one other detail that kept pushing itself on his notice: of course he had done that service — that was settled; but what *was* that service? He must recall it — he would not go to sleep till he had recalled it; it would make his peace of mind perfect. And so he thought and thought. He thought of a dozen things — possible services, even probable services — but none of them seemed adequate, none of them seemed large enough, none of them seemed worth the money — worth the fortune Goodson had wished he could leave in his will. And besides, he couldn't remember having done them, anyway. Now, then — now, then — what *kind* of a service would it be that would make a man so inordinately grateful? Ah — the saving of his soul! That must be it. Yes, he could remember, now, how he once set himself the task of converting Goodson, and labored at it as much as — he was going to say three months; but upon closer examination it shrunk to a month, then to a week, then to a day, then to nothing. Yes, he remembered now, and with unwelcome vividness, that Goodson had told him to go to thunder and mind his own business — *he* wasn't hankering to follow Hadleyburg to heaven!

So that solution was a failure — he hadn't saved Goodson's soul. Richards was discouraged. Then after a little came another idea: had he saved Goodson's property? No, that wouldn't do — he hadn't any. His life? That is it! Of course. Why, he might have thought of it before. This time he was on the right track, sure. His imagination-mill was hard at work in a minute, now.

Thereafter during a stretch of two exhausting hours he was busy saving Goodson's life. He saved it in all kinds of difficult and perilous ways. In every case he got it saved satisfactorily up to a certain point; then, just as he was beginning to get well persuaded that it had really happened, a troublesome detail would turn up which made the whole thing impossible. As in the matter of drowning, for instance. In that case he had swum out and tugged Goodson ashore in an unconscious state with a great crowd looking on and applauding, but when he had got it all thought out and was just beginning to remember all about it, a whole swarm of disqualifying details arrived on the ground: the town would have known of the circumstance, Mary would have known of it, it would glare like a limelight in his own memory instead of being an inconspicuous service which he had possibly rendered "without knowing its full value." And at this point he remembered that he couldn't swim, anyway.

Ah — *there* was a point which he had been overlooking from the start: it had to be a service which he had rendered "possibly without knowing the full value of it." Why, really, that ought to be an easy hunt — much easier than those others. And sure enough, by and by he found it. Goodson, years and years ago, came near marrying a very sweet and pretty girl, named Nancy Hewitt, but in some way or other the match had been broken off; the girl died, Goodson remained a bachelor, and by and by became a soured one and a frank despiser of the human species. Soon after the girl's death the village found out, or thought it had found out, that she carried a spoonful of negro blood in her veins. Richards worked at these details a good while, and in the end he thought he remembered things concerning them which must have gotten mislaid in his memory through long neglect. He seemed to dimly remember that it was *he* that found out about the negro blood; that it was he that told the village; that the village told Goodson where they got it; that he thus saved Goodson from marrying the tainted girl; that he had done him this great service "without knowing the full value of it," in fact without knowing that he *was* doing it; but that Goodson knew the value of it, and what a narrow escape he had had, and so went to his grave grateful to his benefactor and wishing he had a fortune to leave him. It was all clear and simple now, and the more he went over it the more luminous and certain it grew; and at last, when he nestled to sleep satisfied and happy, he remembered the whole thing just as if it had been yesterday. In fact, he dimly remembered Goodson's *telling* him his gratitude once. Meantime Mary had spent six thousand dollars on a new house for herself and a pair of slippers for her pastor, and then had fallen peacefully to rest.

That same Saturday evening the postman had delivered a letter to each of the other principal citizens — nineteen letters in all. No two of the envelopes were alike, and no two of the superscriptions were in the same hand, but the letters inside were just like each other in every detail but one. They were exact copies of the letter received by Richards — handwriting and all — and were all signed by Stephenson, but in place of Richards' name each receiver's own name appeared.

All night long eighteen principal citizens did what their caste-brother Richards was doing at the same time — they put in their energies trying to remember what notable service it was that they had unconsciously done Barclay Goodson. In no case was it a holiday job; still they succeeded.

And while they were at this work, which was difficult, their wives put in the night spending the money, which was easy. During that one night the nineteen wives spent an average of seven thousand dollars each out of the forty thousand in the sack — a hundred and thirty-three thousand altogether.

Next day there was a surprise for Jack Halliday. He noticed that the faces of the nineteen chief citizens and their wives bore that expression of peaceful and holy happiness again. He could not understand it, neither was he able to invent any remarks about it that could damage it or disturb it. And so it was his turn to be dissatisfied with life. His private guesses at the reasons for the happiness failed in all instances, upon examination. When he met Mrs. Wilcox and noticed the placid ecstasy in her face, he said to himself, "Her cat has had kittens" — and went and asked the cook: it was not so; the cook had detected the happiness, but did not know the cause. When Halliday found the duplicate ecstasy in the face of "Shadbelly" Billson (village nickname), he was sure some neighbor of Billson's had broken his leg, but inquiry showed that this had not happened. The subdued ecstasy in Gregory Yates's face could mean but one thing — he was a mother-in-law short: it was another mistake. "And Pinkerton — Pinkerton — he has collected ten cents that he thought he was going to lose." And so on, and so on. In some cases the guesses had to remain in doubt, in the others they proved distinct errors. In the end Halliday said to himself, "Anyway it foots up that there's nineteen Hadleyburg families temporarily in heaven: I don't know how it happened; I only know Providence is off duty today."

An architect and builder from the next state had lately

ventured to set up a small business in this unpromising village, and his sign had now been hanging out a week. Not a
customer yet; he was a discouraged man, and sorry he had
come. But his weather changed suddenly now. First one and
then another chief citizen's wife said to him privately:

"Come to my house Monday week — but say nothing
about it for the present. We think of building."

He got eleven invitations that day. That night he wrote
his daughter and broke off her match with her student. He
said she could marry a mile higher than that.

Pinkerton the banker and two or three other well-to-do
men planned country-seats — but waited. That kind don't
count their chickens until they are hatched.

The Wilsons devised a grand new thing — a fancy-dress
ball. They made no actual promises, but told all their ac-
quaintanceship in confidence that they were thinking the
matter over and thought they should give it — "and if we
do, you will be invited, of course." People were surprised,
and said, one to another, "Why, they are crazy, those poor
Wilsons, they can't afford it." Several among the nineteen
said privately to their husbands, "It is a good idea: we will
keep still till their cheap thing is over, then *we* will give one
that will make it sick."

The days drifted along, and the bill of future squander-
ings rose higher and higher, wilder and wilder, more and
more foolish and reckless. It began to look as if every member of the nineteen would not only spend his whole forty
thousand dollars before receiving-day, but be actually in
debt by the time he got the money. In some cases light-
headed people did not stop with planning to spend, they really spent — on credit. They bought land, mortgages,
farms, speculative stocks, fine clothes, horses, and various
other things, paid down the bonus, and made themselves li-
able for the rest — at ten days. Presently the sober second

thought came, and Halliday noticed that a ghastly anxiety was beginning to show up in a good many faces. Again he was puzzled, and didn't know what to make of it. "The Wilcox kittens aren't dead, for they weren't born; nobody's broken a leg; there's no shrinkage in mother-in-laws; *nothing* has happened — it is an unsolvable mystery."

There was another puzzled man, too — the Rev. Mr. Burgess. For days, wherever he went, people seemed to follow him or to be watching out for him; and if he ever found himself in a retired spot, a member of the nineteen would be sure to appear, thrust an envelope privately into his hand, whisper "To be opened at the town-hall Friday evening," then vanish away like a guilty thing. He was expecting that there might be one claimant for the sack — doubtful, however, Goodson being dead — but it never occurred to him that all this crowd might be claimants. When the great Friday came at last, he found that he had nineteen envelopes.

3

The town-hall had never looked finer. The platform at the end of it was backed by a showy draping of flags; at intervals along the walls were festoons of flags; the gallery fronts were clothed in flags; the supporting columns were swathed in flags; all this was to impress the stranger, for he would be there in considerable force, and in a large degree he would be connected with the press. The house was full. The 412 fixed seats were occupied; also the 68 extra chairs which had been packed into the aisles; the steps of the platform were occupied; some distinguished strangers were given seats on the platform; at the horseshoe of tables which fenced the front and sides of the platform sat a strong force of special correspondents who had come from everywhere.

It was the best-dressed house the town had ever produced. There were some tolerably expensive toilets there, and in several cases the ladies who wore them had the look of being unfamiliar with that kind of clothes. At least the town thought they had that look, but the notion could have arisen from the town's knowledge of the fact that these ladies had never inhabited such clothes before.

The gold-sack stood on a little table at the front of the platform where all the house could see it. The bulk of the house gazed at it with a burning interest, a mouth-watering interest, a wistful and pathetic interest; a minority of nineteen couples gazed at it tenderly, lovingly, proprietarily, and the male half of this minority kept saying over to themselves the moving little impromptu speeches of thankfulness for the audience's applause and congratulations which they were presently going to get up and deliver. Every now and then one of these got a piece of paper out of his vest pocket and privately glanced at it to refresh his memory.

Of course there was a buzz of conversation going on — there always is; but at last when the Rev. Mr. Burgess rose and laid his hand on the sack he could hear his microbes gnaw, the place was so still. He related the curious history of the sack, then went on to speak in warm terms of Hadleyburg's old and well-earned reputation for spotless honesty, and of the town's just pride in this reputation. He said that this reputation was a treasure of priceless value; that under Providence its value had now become inestimably enhanced, for the recent episode had spread this fame far and wide, and thus had focused the eyes of the American world upon this village, and made its name for all time, as he hoped and believed, a synonym for commercial incorruptibility. [*Applause.*] "And who is to be the guardian of this noble treasure — the community as a whole? No!

The responsibility is individual, not communal. From this day forth each and every one of you is in his own person its special guardian, and individually responsible that no harm shall come to it. Do you — does each of you — accept this great trust? [*Tumultuous assent.*] Then all is well. Transmit it to your children and to your children's children. To-day your purity is beyond reproach — see to it that it shall remain so. To-day there is not a person in your community who could be beguiled to touch a penny not his own — see to it that you abide in this grace. [*"We will! we will!"*] This is not the place to make comparisons between ourselves and other communities — some of them ungracious toward us; they have their ways, we have ours; let us be content. [*Applause.*] I am done. Under my hand, my friends, rests a stranger's eloquent recognition of what we are; through him the world will always henceforth know what we are. We do not know who he is, but in your name I utter your gratitude, and ask you to raise your voices in indorsement."

The house rose in a body and made the walls quake with the thunders of its thankfulness for the space of a long minute. Then it sat down, and Mr. Burgess took an envelope out of his pocket. The house held its breath while he slit the envelope open and took from it a slip of paper. He read its contents — slowly and impressively — the audience listening with tranced attention to this magic document, each of whose words stood for an ingot of gold:

" *'The remark which I made to the distressed stranger was this. "You are very far from being a bad man: go, and reform." '* " Then he continued:

"We shall know in a moment now whether the remark here quoted corresponds with the one concealed in the sack; and if that shall prove to be so — and it undoubtedly will — this sack of gold belongs to a fellow-citizen who will henceforth stand before the nation as the symbol of the special virtue which has made our town famous throughout the land — Mr. Billson!"

The house had gotten itself all ready to burst into the proper tornado of applause; but instead of doing it, it seemed stricken with a paralysis; there was a deep hush for a moment or two, then a wave of whispered murmurs swept the place — of about this tenor: *"Billson!* oh, come, this is *too* thin! Twenty dollars to a stranger — or *anybody* — *Billson!* tell it to the marines!" And now at this point the house caught its breath all of a sudden in a new access of astonishment, for it discovered that whereas in one part of the hall Deacon Billson was standing up with his head meekly bowed, in another part of it Lawyer Wilson was doing the same. There was a wondering silence now for a while.

Everybody was puzzled, and nineteen couples were surprised and indignant.

Billson and Wilson turned and stared at each other. Billson asked, bitingly:

"Why do *you* rise, Mr. Wilson?"

"Because I have a right to. Perhaps you will be good enough to explain to the house why *you* rise?"

"With great pleasure. Because I wrote that paper."

"It is an impudent falsity! I wrote it myself."

It was Burgess's turn to be paralyzed. He stood looking vacantly at first one of the men and then the other, and did not seem to know what to do. The house was stupefied. Lawyer Wilson spoke up, now, and said,

"I ask the Chair to read the name signed to that paper."

That brought the Chair to itself, and it read out the name:

" 'John Wharton *Billson*.' "

"There!" shouted Billson, "what have you got to say for

yourself, now? And what kind of apology are you going to make to me and to this insulted house for the imposture which you have attempted to play here?"

"No apologies are due, sir; and as for the rest of it, I publicly charge you with pilfering my note from Mr. Burgess and substituting a copy of it signed with your own name. There is no other way by which you could have gotten hold of the test-remark; I alone, of living men, possessed the secret of its wording."

There was likely to be a scandalous state of things if this went on; everybody noticed with distress that the short-hand scribes were scribbling like mad; many people were crying "Chair, Chair! Order! order!" Burgess rapped with his gavel, and said:

"Let us not forget the proprieties due. There has evidently been a mistake somewhere, but surely that is all. If Mr. Wilson gave me an envelope — and I remember now that he did — I still have it."

He took one out of his pocket, opened it, glanced at it, looked surprised and worried, and stood silent a few moments. Then he waved his hand in a wandering and mechanical way, and made an effort or two to say something, then gave it up, despondently. Several voices cried out:

"Read it! read it! What is it?"

So he began in a dazed and sleep-walker fashion:

" *The remark which I made to the unhappy stranger was this: "You are far from being a bad man.* [The house gazed at him, marveling.] *Go, and reform."* ' [Murmurs: "Amazing! what can this mean?"] This one," said the Chair, "is signed Thurlow G. Wilson."

"There!" cried Wilson. "I reckon that settles it! I knew perfectly well my note was purloined."

"Purloined!" retorted Billson. "I'll let you know that neither you nor any man of your kidney must venture to — "

THE CHAIR "Order, gentlemen, order! Take your seats, both of you, please."

They obeyed, shaking their heads and grumbling angrily. The house was profoundly puzzled; it did not know what to do with this curious emergency. Presently Thompson got up. Thompson was the hatter. He would have liked to be a Nineteener; but such was not for him: his stock of hats was not considerable enough for the position. He said:

"Mr. Chairman, if I may be permitted to make a suggestion, can both of these gentlemen be right? I put it to you, sir, can both have happened to say the very same words to the stranger? It seems to me — "

The tanner got up and interrupted him. The tanner was a disgruntled man; he believed himself entitled to be a Nineteener, but he couldn't get recognition. It made him a little unpleasant in his ways and speech. Said he:

"Sho, *that's* not the point! *That* could happen — twice in a hundred years — but not the other thing. *Neither* of them gave the twenty dollars!"

[*A ripple of applause.*]

BILLSON "*I* did!"

WILSON "*I* did!"

Then each accused the other of pilfering.

THE CHAIR "Order! Sit down, if you please — both of you. Neither of the notes has been out of my possession at any moment."

A VOICE "Good — that settles *that!*"

THE TANNER "Mr. Chairman, one thing is now plain: one of these men have been eavesdropping under the other one's bed, and filching family secrets. If it is not unparliamentary to suggest it, I will remark that both are equal to it. [*The Chair.* "Order! order!"] I withdraw the remark, sir, and will confine myself to suggesting that *if* one of them has overheard the other reveal the test-remark to his wife, we shall catch him now."

A VOICE "How?"

THE TANNER "Easily. The two have not quoted the remark in exactly the same words. You would have noticed that, if there hadn't been a considerable stretch of time and an exciting quarrel inserted between the two readings."

A VOICE "Name the difference."

THE TANNER "The word *very* is in Billson's note, and not in the other."

MANY VOICES "That's so — he's right!"

THE TANNER "And so, if the Chair will examine the test-remark in the sack, we shall know which of these two frauds — [*The Chair.* "Order!"] — which of these two adventurers — [*The Chair.* "Order! order!"] — which of these two gentlemen — [*laughter and applause*] — is entitled to wear the belt as being the first dishonest blatherskite ever bred in this town — which he has dishonored, and which will be a sultry place for him from now out!" [*Vigorous applause.*]

MANY VOICES "Open it! — open the sack!"

Mr. Burgess made a slit in the sack, slid his hand in and brought out an envelope. In it were a couple of folded notes. He said:

"One of these is marked, 'Not to be examined until all written communications which have been addressed to the Chair — if any — shall have been read.' The other is marked 'The Test.' Allow me. It is worded — to wit:

" 'I do not require that the first half of the remark which was made to me by my benefactor shall be quoted with exactness, for it was not striking, and could be forgotten; but its closing fifteen words are quite striking, and I think easily rememberable; unless *these* shall be accurately reproduced, let the applicant be regarded as an impostor. My benefactor began by saying he seldom gave advice to any one, but that it always bore the hall-mark of high value when he did give it. Then he said this — and it has never faded from my memory: *"You are far from being a bad man —* " ' "

FIFTY VOICES "That settles it — the money's Wilson's! Wilson! Wilson! Speech! Speech!"

People jumped up and crowded around Wilson, wringing his hand and congratulating fervently — meantime the Chair was hammering with the gavel and shouting:

"Order, gentlemen! Order! Order! Let me finish reading, please." When quiet was restored, the reading was resumed — as follows:

" ' "*Go, and reform — or, mark my words — some day, for your sins, you will die and go to hell or Hadleyburg —* TRY AND MAKE IT THE FORMER." ' "

A ghastly silence followed. First an angry cloud began to settle darkly upon the faces of the citizenship; after a pause the cloud began to rise, and a tickled expression tried to take its place; tried so hard that it was only kept under with great and painful difficulty; the reporters, the Brixtonites, and other strangers bent their heads down and shielded their faces with their hands, and managed to hold in by main strength and heroic courtesy. At this most inopportune time burst upon the stillness the roar of a solitary voice — Jack Halliday's:

"*That's* got the hall-mark on it!"

Then the house let go, strangers and all. Even Mr. Burgess's gravity broke down presently, then the audience considered itself officially absolved from all restraint, and it made the most of its privilege. It was a good long laugh, and a tempestuously whole-hearted one, but it ceased at last —

g enough for Mr. Burgess to try to resume, and for the
le to get their eyes partially wiped; then it broke out

again; and afterward yet again; then at last Burgess was able to get out these serious words:

"It is useless to try to disguise the fact — we find ourselves in the presence of a matter of grave import. It involves the honor of your town, it strikes at the town's good name. The difference of a single word between the test-remarks offered by Mr. Wilson and Mr. Billson was itself a serious thing, since it indicated that one or the other of these gentlemen had committed a theft — "

The two men were sitting limp, nerveless, crushed; but at these words both were electrified into movement, and started to get up —

"Sit down!" said the Chair, sharply, and they obeyed. "That, as I have said, was a serious thing. And it was — but for only one of them. But the matter has become graver; for the honor of *both* is now in formidable peril. Shall I go even further, and say in inextricable peril? *Both* left out the crucial fifteen words." He paused. During several moments he allowed the pervading stillness to gather and deepen its impressive effects, then added: "There would seem to be but one way whereby this could happen. I ask these gentlemen — Was there *collusion? — agreement?*"

A low murmur sifted through the house; its import was, "He's got them both."

Billson was not used to emergencies; he sat in a helpless collapse. But Wilson was a lawyer. He struggled to his feet, pale and worried, and said:

"I ask the indulgence of the house while I explain this most painful matter. I am sorry to say what I am about to say, since it must inflict irreparable injury upon Mr. Billson, whom I have always esteemed and respected until now, and in whose invulnerability to temptation I entirely believed — as did you all. But for the preservation of my own honor I must speak — and with frankness. I confess with shame

— and I now beseech your pardon for it — that I said to
the ruined stranger all of the words contained in the test-
remark, including the disparaging fifteen. [*Sensation.*]
When the late publication was made I recalled them, and I
resolved to claim the sack of coin, for by every right I was
entitled to it. Now I will ask you to consider this point, and
weigh it well: that stranger's gratitude to me that night
knew no bounds; he said himself that he could find no
words for it that were adequate, and that if he should ever
be able he would repay me a thousandfold. Now, then, I ask
you this: Could I expect — could I believe — could I even
remotely imagine — that, feeling as he did, he would do so
ungrateful a thing as to add those quite unnecessary fifteen
words to his test? — set a trap for me? — expose me as a
slanderer of my own town before my own people assembled
in a public hall? It was preposterous; it was impossible. His
test would contain only the kindly opening clause of my remark. Of that I had no shadow of doubt. You would have
thought as I did. You would not have expected a base be-
trayal from one whom you had befriended and against
whom you had committed no offense. And so, with perfect
confidence, perfect trust, I wrote on a piece of paper the
opening words — ending with 'Go, and reform,' — and
signed it. When I was about to put it in an envelope I was
called into my back office, and without thinking I left the
paper lying open on my desk." He stopped, turned his head
slowly toward Billson, waited a moment, then added: "I ask
you to note this: when I returned, a little later, Mr. Billson
was retiring by my street door." [*Sensation.*]

In a moment Billson was on his feet and shouting:

"It's a lie! It's an infamous lie!"

THE CHAIR "Be seated, sir! Mr. Wilson has the floor."

Billson's friends pulled him into his seat and quieted
him, and Wilson went on:

"Those are the simple facts. My note was now lying in a different place on the table from where I had left it. I noticed that, but attached no importance to it, thinking a draught had blown it there. That Mr. Billson would read a private paper was a thing which could not occur to me; he was a honorable man, and he would be above that. If you will allow me to say it, I think his extra word *very* stands explained; it is attributable to a defect of memory. I was the only man in the world who could furnish here any detail of the test-remark — by *honorable* means. I have finished."

There is nothing in the world like a persuasive speech to fuddle the mental apparatus and upset the convictions and debauch the emotions of an audience not practised in the tricks and delusions of oratory. Wilson sat down victorious. The house submerged him in tides of approving applause; friends swarmed to him and shook him by the hand and congratulated him, and Billson was shouted down and not allowed to say a word. The Chair hammered and hammered with its gavel, and kept shouting:

"But let us proceed, gentlemen, let us proceed!"

At last there was a measurable degree of quiet, and the hatter said:

"But what is there to proceed with, sir, but to deliver the money?"

VOICES "That's it! That's it! Come forward, Wilson!"

THE HATTER "I move three cheers for Mr. Wilson, Symbol of the special virtue which   "

The cheers burst forth before he could finish; and in the midst of them — and in the midst of the clamor of the gavel also — some enthusiasts mounted Wilson on a big friend's shoulder and were going to fetch him in triumph to the platform. The Chair's voice now rose above the noise —

"Order! To your places! You forget that there is still a document to be read." When quiet had been restored he took up the document, and was going to read it, but laid it down again, saying, "I forgot; this is not to be read until all written communications received by me have first been read." He took an envelope out of his pocket, removed its inclosure, glanced at it — seemed astonished — held it out and gazed at it — stared at it.

Twenty or thirty voices cried out:

"What is it? Read it! read it!"

And he did — slowly, and wondering:

" '*The remark which I made to the stranger* — [*Voices.* "Hello! how's this?"] — *was this: "You are far from being a bad man."* [*Voices.* "Great Scott!"] *"Go, and reform."* [*Voices.* "Oh, saw my leg off!"] Signed by Mr. Pinkerton, the banker."

The pandemonium of delight which turned itself loose now was of a sort to make the judicious weep. Those whose withers were unwrung laughed till the tears ran down; the reporters, in throes of laughter, set down disordered pot-hooks which would never in the world be decipherable; and a sleeping dog jumped up, scared out of its wits, and barked itself crazy at the turmoil. All manner of cries were scattered through the din: "We're getting rich — *two* Symbols of Incorruptibility! — without counting Billson!" "*Three!* — count Shadbelly in — we can't have too many!" "All right — Billson's elected!" "Alas, poor Wilson — victim of *two* thieves!"

A POWERFUL VOICE "Silence! The Chair's fishing up something more out of its pocket."

VOICES "Hurrah! Is it something fresh? Read it! read! read!"

THE CHAIR [*reading*] " '*The remark which I made,*' etc.: " '*You are far from being a bad man. "Go,"* ' etc. Signed, 'Gregory Yates.' "

TORNADO OF VOICES "Four Symbols!" "'Rah for Yates!" "Fish again!"

The house was in a roaring humor now, and ready to get all the fun out of the occasion that might be in it. Several Nineteeners, looking pale and distressed, got up and began to work their way toward the aisles, but a score of shouts went up:

"The doors, the doors — close the doors; no Incorruptible shall leave this place! Sit down, everybody!"

The mandate was obeyed.

"Fish again! Read! read!"

The Chair fished again, and once more the familiar words began to fall from its lips — " *'You are far from being a bad man.'* "

"Name! name! What's his name?"

" 'L. Ingoldsby Sargent.' "

"Five elected! Pile up the Symbols! Go on, go on!"

" *'You are far from being a bad —'* "

"Name! name!"

" 'Nicholas Whitworth.' "

"Hooray! hooray! it's a symbolical day!"

Somebody wailed in, and began to sing this rhyme (leaving out "it's") to the lovely "Mikado" tune of "When a man's afraid, a beautiful maid — "; the audience joined in, with joy; then, just in time, somebody contributed another line —

And don't you this forget —

The house roared it out. A third line was at once furnished —

Corruptibles far from Hadleyburg are —

The house roared that one too. As the last note died, Jack
Halliday's voice rose high and clear, freighted with a final
line —

But the Symbols are here, you bet!

That was sung, with booming enthusiasm. Then the happy
house started in at the beginning and sang the four lines
through twice, with immense swing and dash, and finished
up with a crashing three-times-three and a tiger for "Hadleyburg the Incorruptible and all Symbols of it which we
shall find worthy to receive the hall-mark to-night."

Then the shoutings at the Chair began again, all over the
place:

"Go on! go on! Read! read some more! Read all you've
got!"

"That's it — go on! We are winning eternal celebrity!"

A dozen men got up now and began to protest. They said
that this farce was the work of some abandoned joker, and
was an insult to the whole community. Without a doubt
these signatures were all forgeries —

"Sit down! sit down! Shut up! You are confessing. We'll
find *your* names in the lot."

"Mr. Chairman, how many of those envelopes have you
got?"

The Chair counted.

"Together with those that have been already examined,
there are nineteen."

A storm of derisive applause broke out.

"Perhaps they all contain the secret. I move that you
open them all and read every signature that is attached to a
note of that sort — and read also the first eight words of the
note."

"Second the motion!"

It was put and carried — uproariously. Then poor old Richards got up, and his wife rose and stood at his side. Her head was bent down, so that none might see that she was crying. Her husband gave her his arm, and so supporting her, he began to speak in a quavering voice:

"My friends, you have known us two — Mary and me — all our lives, and I think you have liked us and respected us — "

The Chair interrupted him:

"Allow me. It is quite true — that which you are saying, Mr. Richards: this town *does* know you two; it *does* like you; it *does* respect you; more — it honors you and *loves* you — "

Halliday's voice rang out:

"That's the hall-marked truth, too! If the Chair is right, let the house speak up and say it. Rise! Now, then — hip! hip! hip! — all together!"

The house rose in mass, faced toward the old couple eagerly, filled the air with a snow-storm of waving handkerchiefs, and delivered the cheers with all its affectionate heart.

The Chair then continued:

"What I was going to say is this: We know your good heart, Mr. Richards, but this is not a time for the exercise of charity toward offenders. [*Shouts of "Right! right!"*] I see your generous purpose in your face, but I cannot allow you to plead for these men — "

"But I was going to — "

"Please take your seat, Mr. Richards. We must examine the rest of these notes — simple fairness to the men who have already been exposed requires this. As soon as that has been done — I give you my word for this — you shall be heard."

MANY VOICES "Right! — the Chair is right — no interruption can be permitted at this stage! Go on! — the names! the names! — according to the terms of the motion!"

The old couple sat reluctantly down, and the husband whispered to the wife, "It is pitifully hard to have to wait; the shame will be greater than ever when they find we were only going to plead for *ourselves*."

Straightway the jollity broke loose again with the reading of the names.

" '*You are far from being a bad man* — ' Signature, 'Robert J. Titmarsh.'

" '*You are far from being a bad man* — ' Signature, 'Eliphalet Weeks.'

" '*You are far from being a bad man* — ' Signature, 'Oscar B. Wilder.' "

At this point the house lit upon the idea of taking the eight words out of the Chairman's hands. He was not unthankful for that. Thenceforward he held up each note in its turn, and waited. The house droned out the eight words in a massed and measured and musical deep volume of sound (with a daringly close resemblance to a well-known church chant) — " 'You are f-a-r from being a b-a-a-a-d man.' " Then the Chair said, "Signature, 'Archibald Wilcox.' " And so on, and so on, name after name, and everybody had an increasingly and gloriously good time except the wretched Nineteen. Now and then, when a particularly shining name was called, the house made the Chair wait while it chanted the whole of the test-remark from the beginning to the closing words, "And go to hell or Hadleyburg — try and make it the for-or-m-e-r!" and in these special cases they added a grand and agonized and imposing "A-a-a-a-*men!*"

The list dwindled, dwindled, dwindled, poor old Richards keeping tally of the count, wincing when a name resembling his own was pronounced, and waiting in miserable suspense for the time to come when it would be his humiliating privilege to rise with Mary and finish his plea, which he was intending to word thus: ". . . for until now we have never done any wrong thing, but have gone our humble way unreproached. We are very poor, we are old, and have no chick nor child to help us; we were sorely tempted, and we fell. It was my purpose when I got up before to make confession and beg that my name might not be read out in this public place, for it seemed to us that we could not bear it; but I was prevented. It was just; it was our place to suffer with the rest. It has been hard for us. It is the first time we have ever heard our name fall from any one's lips — sullied. Be merciful — for the sake of the better days; make our shame as light to bear as in your charity you can." At this point in his revery Mary nudged him, perceiving that his mind was absent. The house was chanting, "You are f-a-r," etc.

"Be ready," Mary whispered. "Your name comes now; he has read eighteen."

The chant ended.

"Next! next! next!" came volleying from all over the house.

Burgess put his hand into his pocket. The old couple, trembling, began to rise. Burgess fumbled a moment, then said,

"I find I have read them all."

Faint with joy and surprise, the couple sank into their seats, and Mary whispered:

"Oh, bless God, we are saved! — he has lost ours — I wouldn't give this for a hundred of those sacks!"

The house burst out with its "Mikado" travesty, and sang it three times with ever-increasing enthusiasm, rising to its feet when it reached for the third time the closing line —

But the Symbols are here, you bet!

and finishing up with cheers and a tiger for "Hadleyburg purity and our eighteen immortal representatives of it."

Then Wingate, the saddler, got up and proposed cheers "for the cleanest man in town, the one solitary important citizen in it who didn't try to steal that money — Edward Richards."

They were given with great and moving heartiness; then somebody proposed that Richards be elected sole guardian and Symbol of the now Sacred Hadleyburg Tradition, with power and right to stand up and look the whole sarcastic world in the face.

Passed, by acclamation; then they sang the "Mikado" again, and ended it with:

And there's one Symbol left, you bet!

There was a pause; then —

A VOICE "Now, then, who's to get the sack?"

THE TANNER (*with bitter sarcasm*) "That's easy. The money has to be divided among the eighteen Incorruptibles. They gave the suffering stranger twenty dollars apiece — and that remark — each in his turn — it took twenty-two minutes for the procession to move past. Staked the stranger — total contribution, $360. All they want is just the loan back — and interest — forty thousand dollars altogether."

MANY VOICES [*derisively*] "That's it! Divvy! divvy! Be kind to the poor — don't keep them waiting!"

THE CHAIR "Order! I now offer the stranger's remaining document. It says: 'If no claimant shall appear [*grand chorus of groans*] I desire that you open the sack and count out the money to the principal citizens of your town, they to

take it in trust [*cries of "Oh! Oh! Oh!"*], and use it in such
ways as to them shall seem best for the propagation and
preservation of your community's noble reputation for incorruptible honesty [*more cries*] — a reputation to which
their names and their efforts will add a new and far-
reaching luster.' [*Enthusiastic outburst of sarcastic applause.*]
That seems to be all. No — here is a postscript:

'P. S. — CITIZENS OF HADLEYBURG: *There is no test-remark
— nobody made one.* [Great sensation.] *There wasn't any
pauper stranger, nor any twenty-dollar contribution, nor any
accompanying benediction and compliment — these are all
inventions.* [General buzz and hum of astonishment and delight.] *Allow me to tell my story — it will take but a word or
two. I passed through your town at a certain time, and received a deep offense which I had not earned. Any other man
would have been content to kill one or two of you and call it
square, but to me that would have been a trivial revenge, and
inadequate; for the dead do not suffer. Besides, I could not kill
you all — and, anyway, made as I am, even that would not
have satisfied me. I wanted to damage every man in the place,
and every woman — and not in their bodies or in their estate,
but in their vanity — the place where feeble and foolish people
are most vulnerable. So I disguised myself and came back and
studied you. You were easy game. You had an old and lofty reputation for honesty, and naturally you were proud of it — it
was your treasure of treasures, the very apple of your eye. As
soon as I found out that you carefully and vigilantly kept yourselves and your children out of temptation, I knew how to
proceed. Why, you simple creatures, the weakest of all weak
things is a virtue which has not been tested in the fire. I laid a
plan, and gathered a list of names. My project was to corrupt
Hadleyburg the Incorruptible. My idea was to make liars and
thieves of nearly half a hundred smirchless men and women*

*who had never in their lives uttered a lie or stolen a penny. I
was afraid of Goodson. He was neither born nor reared in
Hadleyburg. I was afraid that if I started to operate my scheme
by getting my letter laid before you, you would say to yourselves,
"Goodson is the only man among us who would give away
twenty dollars to a poor devil"—and then you might not bite
at my bait. But Heaven took Goodson; then I knew I was safe,
and I set my trap and baited it. It may be that I shall not catch
all the men to whom I mailed the pretended test secret, but I
shall catch the most of them, if I know Hadleyburg nature.
[Voices. "Right—he got every last one of them."] I believe
they will even steal ostensible gamble-money, rather than miss,
poor, tempted, and mistrained fellows. I am hoping to eternally
and everlastingly squelch your vanity and give Hadleyburg a
new renown—one that will stick—and spread far. If I have
succeeded, open the sack and summon the Committee on Propagation and Preservation of the Hadleyburg Reputation.'*

A CYCLONE OF VOICES "Open it! Open it! The Eighteen
to the front! Committee on Propagation of the Tradition!
Forward — the Incorruptibles!"

The Chair ripped the sack wide, and gathered up a handful of bright, broad, yellow coins, shook them together,
then examined them —

"Friends, they are only gilded disks of lead!"

There was a crashing outbreak of delight over this news,
and when the noise had subsided, the tanner called out:

"By right of apparent seniority in this business, Mr. Wilson is Chairman of the Committee on Propagation of the
Tradition. I suggest that he step forward on behalf of his
pals, and receive in trust the money."

A HUNDRED VOICES "Wilson! Wilson! Wilson! Speech!
Speech!"

WILSON [*in a voice trembling with anger*] "You will allow

me to say, and without apologies for my language, *damn* the money!"

A VOICE "Oh, and him a Baptist!"

A VOICE "Seventeen Symbols left! Step up, gentlemen, and assume your trust!"

There was a pause — no response.

THE SADDLER "Mr. Chairman, we've got *one* clean man left, anyway, out of the late aristocracy; and he needs money, and deserves it. I move that you appoint Jack Halliday to get up there and auction off that sack of gilt twenty-dollar pieces, and give the result to the right man — the man whom Hadleyburg delights to honor — Edward Richards."

This was received with great enthusiasm, the dog taking a hand again; the saddler started the bids at a dollar, the Brixton folk and Barnum's representative fought hard for it, the people cheered every jump that the bids made, the excitement climbed moment by moment higher and higher, the bidders got on their mettle and grew steadily more and more daring, more and more determined, the jumps went from a dollar up to five, then to ten, then to twenty, then fifty, then to a hundred, then —

At the beginning of the auction Richards whispered in distress to his wife: "O Mary, can we allow it? It — it — you see, it is an honor-reward, a testimonial to purity of character, and — and — can we allow it? Hadn't I better get up and — O Mary, what ought we to do? — what do you think we — [*Halliday's voice. "Fifteen I'm bid! — fifteen for the sack! — twenty! — ah, thanks! — thirty — thanks again! Thirty, thirty, thirty! — do I heard forty? — forty it is! Keep the ball rolling, gentlemen, keep it rolling! — fifty! thanks, noble Roman! going at fifty, fifty, fifty! — seventy! — ninety! — splendid! — a hundred! — pile it up, pile it up! — hundred and twenty — forty! — just in time! — hundred*

and fifty! — TWO *hundred!* — *superb! Do I hear two h* —
thanks! — *two hundred and fifty!* — "]

"It is another temptation, Edward — I'm all in a tremble
— but, oh, we've escaped *one* temptation, and that ought
to warn us to — [*"Six did I hear?* — *thanks!* — *six-fifty,
six-f* — SEVEN *hundred!"*] And yet, Edward, when you think
— nobody susp — [*"Eight hundred dollars!* — *hurrah!* —
make it nine! — *Mr. Parsons, did I hear you say* — *thanks* —
nine! — *this noble sack of virgin lead going at only nine hundred dollars, gilding and all* — *come! do I hear* — *a thousand!* — *gratefully yours!* — *did some one say eleven?* — *a
sack which is going to be the most celebrated in the whole Uni*
—] O Edward" (beginning to sob), "we are *so* poor! — but
— but — do as you think best — do as you think best."

Edward fell — that is, he sat still; sat with a conscience
which was not satisfied, but which was overpowered by circumstances.

Meantime a stranger, who looked like an amateur detec-
tive gotten up as an impossible English earl, had been
watching the evening's proceedings with manifest interest,
and with a contented expression in his face; and he had
been privately commenting to himself. He was now solilo-
quizing somewhat like this: "None of the Eighteen are bidding; that is not satisfactory; I must change that — the
dramatic unities require it; they must buy the sack they
tried to steal; they must pay a heavy price, too — some of
them are rich. And another thing, when I make a mistake
in Hadleyburg nature the man that puts that error upon me
is entitled to a high honorarium, and some one must pay it.
This poor old Richards has brought my judgment to
shame; he is an honest man: — I don't understand it, but I
acknowledge it. Yes, he saw my deuces *and* with a straight
flush, and by rights the pot is his. And it shall be a jack-pot,

too, if I can manage it. He disappointed me, but let that pass."

He was watching the bidding. At a thousand, the market broke; the prices tumbled swiftly. He waited — and still watched. One competitor dropped out; then another, and another. He put in a bid or two, now. When the bids had sunk to ten dollars, he added a five; some one raised him a three; he waited a moment, then flung in a fifty-dollar jump, and the sack was his — at $1,282. The house broke out in cheers — then stopped; for he was on his feet, and had lifted his hand. He began to speak.

"I desire to say a word, and ask a favor. I am a speculator in rarities, and I have dealings with persons interested in numismatics all over the world. I can make a profit on this purchase, just as it stands; but there is a way, if I can get your approval, whereby I can make every one of these leaden twenty-dollar pieces worth its face in gold, and perhaps more. Grant me that approval, and I will give part of my gains to your Mr. Richards, whose invulnerable probity you have so justly and so cordially recognized to-night; his share shall be ten thousand dollars, and I will hand him the money to-morrow. [*Great applause from the house.* But the "invulnerable probity" made the Richardses blush prettily; however, it went for modesty, and did no harm.] If you will pass my proposition by a good majority — I would like a two-thirds vote — I will regard that as the town's consent, and that is all I ask. Rarities are always helped by any device which will rouse curiosity and compel remark. Now if I may have your permission to stamp upon the faces of each of these ostensible coins the names of the eighteen gentlemen who — "

Nine-tenths of the audience were on their feet in a moment — dog and all — and the proposition was carried with a whirlwind of approving applause and laughter.

They sat down, and all the Symbols except "Dr." Clay Harkness got up, violently protesting against the proposed outrage, and threatening to —

"I beg you not to threaten me," said the stranger, calmly. "I know my legal rights, and am not accustomed to being frightened at bluster." [*Applause.*] He sat down. "Dr." Harkness saw an opportunity here. He was one of the two very rich men of the place, and Pinkerton was the other. Harkness was proprietor of a mint; that is to say, a popular patent medicine. He was running for the legislature on one ticket, and Pinkerton on the other. It was a close race and a hot one, and getting hotter every day. Both had strong appetites for money; each had bought a great tract of land, with a purpose; there was going to be a new railway, and each wanted to be in the legislature and help locate the route to his own advantage; a single vote might make the decision, and with it two or three fortunes. The stake was large, and Harkness was a daring speculator. He was sitting close to the stranger. He leaned over while one or another of the other Symbols was entertaining the house with protests and appeals, and asked, in a whisper.

"What is your price for the sack?"

"Forty thousand dollars."

"I'll give you twenty."

"No."

"Twenty-five."

"No."

"Say thirty."

"The price is forty thousand dollars; not a penny less."

"All right, I'll give it. I will come to the hotel at ten in the morning. I don't want it known: will see you privately."

"Very good." Then the stranger got up and said to the house:

"I find it late. The speeches of these gentlemen are not without merit, not without interest, not without grace; yet if I may be excused I will take my leave. I thank you for the great favor which you have shown me in granting my petition. I ask the Chair to keep the sack for me until tomorrow, and to hand these three five-hundred-dollar notes to Mr. Richards." They were passed up to the Chair. "At nine I will call for the sack, and at eleven will deliver the rest of the ten thousand to Mr. Richards in person, at his home. Good night."

Then he slipped out, and left the audience making a vast noise which was composed of a mixture of cheers, the "Mikado" song, dog-disapproval, and the chant, "You are f-a-r from being a b-a-a-d man — a-a-a-a-men!"

4

At home the Richardses had to endure congratulations and compliments until midnight. Then they were left to themselves. They looked a little sad, and they sat silent and thinking. Finally Mary sighed and said,

"Do you think we are to blame, Edward — *much* to blame?" and her eyes wandered to the accusing triplet of big banknotes lying on the table, where the congratulators had been gloating over them and reverently fingering them. Edward did not answer at once; then he brought out a sigh and said, hesitatingly:

"We — we couldn't help it, Mary. It — well, it was ordered. *All* things are."

Mary glanced up and looked at him steadily, but he didn't return the look. Presently she said:

"I thought congratulations and praises always tasted good. But — it seems to me, now — Edward?"

"Well?"

"Are you going to stay in the bank?"

"N-no."

"Resign?"

"In the morning — by note."

"It does seem best."

Richards bowed his head in his hands and muttered:

"Before, I was not afraid to let oceans of people's money pour through my hands, but — Mary, I am so tired, so tired — "

"We will go to bed."

At nine in the morning the stranger called for the sack and took it to the hotel in a cab. At ten Harkness had a talk with him privately. The stranger asked for and got five checks on a metropolitan bank — drawn to "Bearer" — four for $1,500 each, and one for $34,000. He put one of the former in his pocketbook, and the remainder, representing $38,500, he put in an envelope, and with these he added a note, which he wrote after Harkness was gone. At eleven he called at the Richards house and knocked. Mrs. Richards peeped through the shutters, then went and received the envelope, and the stranger disappeared without a word. She came back flushed and a little unsteady on her legs, and gasped out:

"I am sure I recognized him! Last night it seemed to me that maybe I had seen him somewhere before."

"He is the man that brought the sack here?"

"I am almost sure of it."

"Then he is the ostensible Stephenson, too, and sold every important citizen in this town with his bogus secret. Now if he has sent checks instead of money, we are sold, too, after we thought we had escaped. I was beginning to feel fairly comfortable once more, after my night's rest, but the look of that envelope makes me sick. It isn't fat enough;

$8,500 in even the largest bank-notes makes more bulk than that."

"Edward, why do you object to checks?"

"Checks signed by Stephenson! I am resigned to take the $8,500 if it could come in bank-notes — for it does seem that it was so ordered, Mary — but I have never had much courage, and I have not the pluck to try to market a check signed with that disastrous name. It would be a trap. That man tried to catch me; we escaped somehow or other; and now he is trying a new way. If it is checks — "

"Oh, Edward, it is *too* bad!" and she held up the checks and began to cry.

"Put them in the fire! quick! we mustn't be tempted. It is a trick to make the world laugh at *us*, along with the rest, and — Give them to *me*, since you can't do it!" He snatched them and tried to hold his grip till he could get to the stove; but he was human, he was a cashier, and he stopped a moment to make sure of the signature. Then he came near to fainting.

"Fan me, Mary, fan me! They are the same as gold!"

"Oh, how lovely, Edward! Why?"

"Signed by Harkness. What can the mystery of that be, Mary?"

"Edward, do you think — "

"Look here — look at this! Fifteen — fifteen — fifteen — thirty-four. Thirty-eight thousand five hundred! Mary, the sack isn't worth twelve dollars, and Harkness — apparently — has paid about par for it."

"And does it all come to us, do you think — instead of the ten thousand?"

"Why, it looks like it. And the checks are made to 'Bearer,' too."

"Is that good, Edward? What is it for?"

"A hint to collect them at some distant bank, I reckon.

Perhaps Harkness doesn't want the matter known. What is that — a note?"

"Yes. It was with the checks."

It was in the "Stephenson" handwriting, but there was no signature. It said:

"I am a disappointed man. Your honesty is beyond the reach of temptation. I had a different idea about it, but I wronged you in that, and I beg pardon, and do it sincerely. I honor you — and that is sincere too. This town is not worthy to kiss the hem of your garment. Dear sir, I made a square bet with myself that there were nineteen debauchable men in your self-righteous community. I have lost. Take the whole pot, you are entitled to it."

Richards drew a deep sigh, and said:

"It seems written with fire — it burns so. Mary — I am miserable again."

"I, too. Ah, dear, I wish — "

"To think, Mary — he *believes* in me."

"Oh, don't, Edward — I can't bear it."

"If those beautiful words were deserved, Mary — and God knows I believed I deserved them once — I think I could give the forty thousand dollars for them. And I would put that paper away, as representing more than gold and jewels, and keep it always. But now — We could not live in the shadow of its accusing presence, Mary."

He put it in the fire.

A messenger arrived and delivered an envelope.

Richards took from it a note and read it; it was from Burgess.

"You saved me, in a difficult time. I saved you last night. It was at cost of a lie, but I made the sacrifice freely, and out of a

grateful heart. None in this village knows so well as I know how brave and good and noble you are. At bottom you cannot respect me, knowing as you do of that matter of which I am accused, and by the general voice condemned; but I beg that you will at least believe that I am a grateful man; it will help me to bear my burden."

[*Signed*] BURGESS

"Saved, once more. And on such terms!" He put the note in the fire. "I — I wish I were dead, Mary, I wish I were out of it all."

"Oh, these are bitter, bitter days, Edward. The stabs, through their very generosity, are so deep — and they come so fast!"

Three days before the election each of two thousand voters suddenly found himself in possession of a prized memento — one of the renowned bogus double-eagles. Around one of its faces was stamped these words: "THE REMARK I MADE TO THE POOR STRANGER WAS — " Around the other face was stamped these: "GO, AND REFORM. [SIGNED] PINKERTON." Thus the entire remaining refuse of the renowned joke was emptied upon a single head, and with calamitous effect. It revived the recent vast laugh and concentrated it upon Pinkerton; and Harkness's election was a walkover.

Within twenty-four hours after the Richardses had received their checks their consciences were quieting down, discouraged; the old couple were learning to reconcile themselves to the sin which they had committed. But they were to learn, now, that a sin takes on new and real terrors when there seems a chance that it is going to be found out. This gives it a fresh and most substantial and important aspect. At church the morning sermon was of the usual pattern; it was the same old things said in the same old way;

they had heard them a thousand times and found them in-
nocuous, next to meaningless, and easy to sleep under; but
now it was different: the sermon seemed to bristle with ac-
cusations; it seemed aimed straight and specially at people
who were concealing deadly sins. After church they got
away from the mob of congratulators as soon as they could,
and hurried homeward, chilled to the bone at they did not
know what — vague, shadowy, indefinite fears. And by
chance they caught a glimpse of Mr. Burgess as he turned a
corner. He paid no attention to their nod of recognition!
He hadn't seen it; but they did not know that. What could
his conduct mean? It might mean — it might mean — oh,
a dozen dreadful things. Was it possible that he knew that
Richards could have cleared him of guilt in that bygone
time, and had been silently waiting for a chance to even up
accounts? At home, in their distress they got to imagining
that their servant might have been in the next room listening when Richards revealed the secret to his wife that he
knew of Burgess's innocence; next, Richards began to imagine that he had heard the swish of a gown in there at that
time; next, he was sure he *had* heard it. They would call
Sarah in, on a pretext, and watch her face: if she had been
betraying them to Mr. Burgess, it would show in her manner. They asked her some questions — questions which
were so random and incoherent and seemingly purposeless
that the girl felt sure that the old people's minds had been
affected by their sudden good fortune; the sharp and watch-
ful gaze which they bent upon her frightened her, and that
completed the business. She blushed, she became nervous
and confused, and to the old people these were plain signs
of guilt — guilt of some fearful sort or other — without
doubt she was a spy and a traitor. When they were alone
again they began to piece many unrelated things together
and get horrible results out of the combination. When

things had got about to the worst, Richards was delivered of a sudden gasp, and his wife asked:

"Oh, what is it? — what is it?"

"The note — Burgess's note! Its language was sarcastic, I see it now." He quoted: " 'At bottom you cannot respect me, *knowing*, as you do, of *that matter* of which I am accused' — oh, it is perfectly plain, now, God help me! He knows that I know! You see the ingenuity of the phrasing. It was a trap — and like a fool, I walked into it. And Mary — ?"

"Oh, it is dreadful — I know what you are going to say — he didn't return your transcript of the pretended test-remark."

"No — kept it to destroy us with. Mary, he has exposed us to some already. I know it — I know it well. I saw it in a dozen faces after church. Ah, he wouldn't answer our nod of recognition — *he* knew what he had been doing!"

In the night the doctor was called. The news went around in the morning that the old couple were rather seriously ill — prostrated by the exhausting excitement growing out of their great windfall, the congratulations, and the late hours, the doctor said. The town was sincerely distressed; for these old people were about all it had left to be proud of, now.

Two days later the news was worse. The old couple were delirious, and were doing strange things. By witness of the nurses, Richards had exhibited checks — for $8,500? No — for an amazing sum — $38,500! What could be the explanation of this gigantic piece of luck?

The following day the nurses had more news — and wonderful. They had concluded to hide the checks, lest harm come to them; but when they searched they were gone from under the patient's pillow — vanished away. The patient said:

"Let the pillow alone; what do you want?"

"We thought it best that the checks — "

"You will never see them again — they are destroyed. They came from Satan. I saw the hell-brand on them, and I knew they were sent to betray me to sin." Then he fell to gabbling strange and dreadful things which were not clearly understandable, and which the doctor admonished them to keep to themselves.

Richards was right; the checks were never seen again.

A nurse must have talked in her sleep, for within two days the forbidden gabblings were the property of the town; and they were of a surprising sort. They seemed to indicate that Richards had been a claimant for the sack himself, and that Burgess had concealed that fact and then maliciously betrayed it.

Burgess was taxed with this and stoutly denied it. And he said it was not fair to attach weight to the chatter of a sick old man who was out of his mind. Still, suspicion was in the air, and there was much talk.

After a day or two it was reported that Mrs. Richards's delirious deliveries were getting to be duplicates of her husband's. Suspicion flamed up into conviction, now, and the town's pride in the purity of its one undiscredited important citizen began to dim down and flicker toward extinction.

Six days passed, then came more news. The old couple were dying. Richards's mind cleared in his latest hour, and sent for Burgess. Burgess said:

"Let the room be cleared. I think he wishes to say something in privacy."

"No!" said Richards: "I want witnesses. I want you all to hear my confession, so that I may die a man, and not a dog. I was clean — artificially — like the rest; and like the rest I fell when temptation came. I signed a lie, and claimed the miserable sack. Mr. Burgess remembered that I had done him a service, and in gratitude (and ignorance) he suppressed my claim and saved me. You know the thing that was charged against Burgess years ago. My testimony, and mine alone, could have cleared him, and I was a coward, and left him to suffer disgrace — "

"No — no — Mr. Richards, you — "

"My servant betrayed my secret to him — "

"No one has betrayed anything to me — "

— "and then he did a natural and justifiable thing, he repented of the saving kindness which he had done me, and he *exposed* me — as I deserved — "

"Never! — I make oath — "

"Out of my heart I forgive him."

Burgess's impassioned protestations fell upon deaf ears; the dying man passed away without knowing that once more he had done poor Burgess a wrong. The old wife died that night.

The last of the sacred Nineteen had fallen a prey to the fiendish sack; the town was stripped of the last rag of its ancient glory. Its mourning was not showy, but it was deep.

By act of the Legislature — upon prayer and petition — Hadleyburg was allowed to change its name to (never mind what — I will not give it away), and leave one word out of the motto that for many generations had graced the town's official seal.

It is an honest town once more, and the man will have to rise early that catches it napping again.

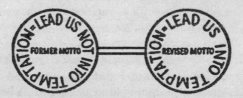

A FABLE

Once upon a time an artist who had painted a small and very beautiful picture placed it so that he could see it in the mirror. He said, "This doubles the distance and softens it, and it is twice as lovely as it was before."

The animals out in the woods heard of this through the housecat, who was greatly admired by them because he was so learned, and so refined and civilized, and so polite and high-bred, and could tell them so much which they didn't know before, and were not certain about afterward. They were much excited about this new piece of gossip, and they asked questions, so as to get at a full understanding of it. They asked what a picture was, and the cat explained.

"It is a flat thing," he said; "wonderfully flat, marvelously flat, enchantingly flat and elegant. And, oh, so beautiful!"

That excited them almost to a frenzy, and they said they would give the world to see it. Then the bear asked:

"What is it that makes it so beautiful?"

"It is the looks of it," said the cat.

This filled them with admiration and uncertainty, and they were more excited than ever. Then the cow asked:

"What is a mirror?"

"It is a hole in the wall," said the cat. "You look in it, and there you see the picture, and it is so dainty and charming and ethereal and inspiring in its unimaginable beauty that your head turns round and round, and you almost swoon with ecstasy."

The ass had not said anything as yet; he now began to throw doubts. He said there had never been anything as beautiful as this before, and probably wasn't now. He said that when it took a whole basketful of sesquipedalian adjectives to whoop up a thing of beauty, it was time for suspicion.

It was easy to see that these doubts were having an effect upon the animals, so the cat went off offended. The subject was dropped for a couple of days, but in the meantime curiosity was taking a fresh start, and there was a revival of interest perceptible. Then the animals assailed the ass for spoiling what could possibly have been a pleasure to them, on a mere suspicion that the picture was not beautiful, without any evidence that such was the case. The ass was not troubled; he was calm, and said there was one way to find out who was in the right, himself or the cat: he would go and look in that hole, and come back and tell what he found there. The animals felt relieved and grateful, and asked him to go at once — which he did.

But he did not know where he ought to stand; and, so, through error, he stood between the picture and the mirror. The result was that the picture had no chance, and didn't show up. He returned home and said:

"The cat lied. There was nothing in that hole but an ass. There wasn't a sign of a flat thing visible. It was a handsome ass, and friendly, but just an ass, and nothing more."

The elephant asked:

"Did you see it good and clear? Were you close to it?"

"I saw it good and clear, O Hathi, King of Beasts. I was so close that I touched noses with it."

"This is very strange," said the elephant; "the cat was always truthful before — as far as we could make out. Let another witness try. Go, Baloo, look in the hole, and come and report."

So the bear went. When he came back, he said:

"Both the cat and the ass have lied; there was nothing in the hole but a bear."

Great was the surprise and puzzlement of the animals. Each was now anxious to make the test himself and get at the straight truth. The elephant sent them one at a time.

First, the cow. She found nothing in the hole but a cow.

The tiger found nothing in it but a tiger.

The lion found nothing in it but a lion.

The leopard found nothing in it but a leopard.

The camel found a camel, and nothing more.

The Hathi was wroth, and said he would have the truth, if he had to go and fetch it himself. When he returned, he abused his whole subjectry for liars, and was in an unappeasable fury with the moral and mental blindness of the cat. He said anybody but a near-sighted fool could see that there was nothing in the hole but an elephant.

MORAL, BY THE CAT

You can find in a text whatever you bring, if you will stand between it and the mirror of your imagination. You may not see your ears, but they will be there.